Clio

A novel by

Elizabeth Fritz

iUniverse LLC
Bloomington

CLIO

iUniverse books may be ordered through booksellers or by contacting:

iUniverse
1663 Liberty Drive
Bloomington, IN 47403
www.iuniverse.com
1-800-Authors (1-800-288-4677)

ISBN: 978-1-4917-1000-5 (sc)

Printed in the United States of America.

iUniverse rev. date: 10/31/2013

Also by Elizabeth Fritz

*Surprise Surprise**

*Cousin Delia's Legacy**

*Hope's Journey**

*Trio**

*Assisted Living—Or Dying**

*Athena**

*Hunting Giovane**

*Prosperity**

*Magnolias and Murder**

*Also available in e-book

For Jean

§ One §

One more long, deep breath of spring-scented air before I opened the door to Hauteville House. A stray sunbeam flashed from the trophy of antique Oriental arms hanging on the paneled wall. Pierce stood waiting at the foot of the stair, slender, straight-backed, his smooth white head like a beacon against the dark wood.

"He's expecting you, Miss Clio," he said.

"Thank you, Pierce. I'm going right up."

On the landing, I met Mrs. Bettle coming out of his room. As she passed me, she said, "I've just given him his medication, Miss Clio; he ought to be asleep very soon."

"Thank you, Mrs. Bettle," I replied and entered his room.

He lay stiff and still as a log on the bed, his eyes open but empty of welcome or any other expression. They lay under his bony brow like faded blue marbles under half-closed lids. The silvery stubble on his cheeks and chin indicated that Pierce had not yet shaved him.

"Good morning, Papa," I said as I sat down on the straight-backed chair at the side of the bed. His lids flickered but there was no more response than that to my greeting.

I folded my hands in my lap and fixed my gaze on them. In a few minutes, his breath slowed and deepened and he slept. I let my mind wander as it had for all the long days I had sat on watch at this bedside, spelled only by Mrs. Bettle during the day and Arnold Slocum during the night hours. We watched in order to respond when he went into a seizure, in order to force the medicine between his clenched teeth or to inject it into his arm, in order to prevent his dying in the seizure. For fifteen years I had been a slave to this mysterious affliction he endured, waiting, watching, while my youth drained away and my *joie de vivre* faded into ashes. I hated him, I hated this life, I hated this house. I was continually struck by the irony that only a slight mispronunciation of its name made it "Hateful House." But I kept the hate carefully hidden under a layer of civility and good manners.

§ Two §

ONCE, IN MY great grandfather's day, the house had been full of hope. Armand Ladurie DeVille was a poverty stricken Quebeçois who emigrated to the States in the latter years of the 19th century, worked hard, managed his assets shrewdly, acquired interests in railroads, forests, and steel mills, and when his growing wealth seemed to justify a grandiose domicile, built Hauteville House. He had married the charming but penniless daughter of a schoolmaster, then provided her with tutors to teach the graces and skills of moneyed society. Hauteville House was an advertisement of Armand and Dora's success—built of cut stone, sprawling, multi-towered, trimmed with handsome carvings and even some gargoyles; its interior was lighted by day by vast expanses of stained and clear glass windows, and by night with that newfangled fad, electricity. Intricately carved wood gleamed darkly on stair rail and balusters, door and window frames, and mantle pieces. Huge, high-vaulted rooms on the first floor were calculated to entertain and impress wealthy friends and business acquaintances, just as the drab, cramped cubicles on the third floor were designed to house the small army of servants required for the DeVille's life style. The buoyant hope and energy of the age was expressed further in lavish draperies, ornate furniture, Oriental carpets—*décor* which vanished in the next age, that of my grandfather Armand LaDurie II. His wife was a pampered only child of a New York investment banker and her taste demanded the banishing of the *fin de siècle* interior trappings of the first floor to the attic of the carriage house. She replaced the old fashion she disdained with the stark lines, shiny surfaces, and vivid colors of Art Deco, changes so far out of keeping with the house's skeleton that Armand II's second wife sent all the Art Deco stuff to a storage room in the cellar. Her choice of furnishings was Post-War overstuffed sofas and chairs and spindle-legged coffee tables. She also grudgingly provided Armand II with Armand Ladurie III (Papa) and then went off to France with alimony sufficiently generous to deplete the cash reserves of both Armand I and II. Papa found it necessary to marry money and my mother, Felicia, filled the bill; she was the cultured heiress to a brewery fortune, with which she and Papa introduced Danish and Swedish Modern rather haphazardly into the House. The result was incongruous but not all bad.

It was in the era of Armand III and Felicia that the House gained me and lost hope. I never knew Felicia except from her portrait in the drawing room; she died when I was three and a succession of nannies, governesses, and tutors reared me with only rare interventions by Papa in the process. Mrs. Ryan said after Felicia died Papa became a recluse, leaving all the management of estate and household to lawyers and servants. He spent his time in the library surrounded by bulky tomes and stacks of manuscript. Educated as a classical scholar, he was expert in four languages, the histories of five ancient civilizations, and geographies of six continents. Papa's life was dedicated to translation of classic literature into modern English; he dismissed the Victorian versions as unreadable. He never published what he translated, just accumulated manuscripts in an enormous armoire in the library. When I was 14 and had demonstrated prowess in French and English, doctors told Papa his eyesight was threatened. Aha, he thought, here's this otherwise useless creature that I can co-opt for my work. At least, that's how I subsequently interpreted his unexpected but not unwelcome interest in me. I didn't hate him then; in fact, I so much loved what he taught me that I didn't miss demonstrations of affection or kindness. He made a stern but thorough taskmaster and by the time I was 20 and had become an accomplished translator and typist, I was so useful to him that he begrudged my daily walks around the grounds or my occasional shopping trips to the village. If it had not been for Pierce, the butler, and Mrs. Ryan, the housekeeper, I would not have had these rare outings or regular medical or dental care.

Just prior to my 21st birthday, the seizures started. For the first few years, they interrupted Papa's work only occasionally and for only short periods of time. Then they came more frequently and lasted longer, finally putting Papa in bed permanently, with a continual watch posted to rescue him from a mortal attack. I slipped into the role of bedside care-giver and watcher, fulfilling what seemed to be my filial duty. To pass the time between my stints at his bedside, I continued with the translations on my own. From then on I was valued as reader of *my* current work; when he could still talk, he would criticize my grammar or syntax or interpretation, and would order up a corrected version at the next watch. After he lost the ability to talk, his expressionless face and fluttering eyelids were the only signs of life and intelligence to be seen. Although I wasn't sure he heard me, I sometimes spoke of my progress or problems with difficult passages. But he no longer acknowledged my voice, much less my presence.

It was after my 35th birthday that I began to hate him.

§ Three §

In May of that year, my birthday fell on a Saturday. Pierce and Mrs. Ryan marked the day for me with a special dinner featuring Beef Wellington, Duchess potatoes, Caesar salad, and German chocolate cake. They tactfully refrained from putting 35 candles on the cake. Pierce served in the dining room as I sat solitary in queenly state at the long table; Mrs. Ryan hovered to ensure observation of proper ceremony. Dinner was pleasantly festive and there were presents—a silver pen from Mrs. Ryan and a velvet cushion for my desk chair from Pierce. I praised the meal and made all the appropriately grateful noises in accepting the gifts. Mrs. Bettle's contribution to the celebration was to take my evening stint at Papa's bedside, freeing me for a walk in the soft spring evening.

I shrugged into a shawl, the spring evening was just a bit nippy, and started out on my usual path. Then, thinking what the hey it's my birthday, I took the long way through the wood to go by the derelict cottage where once a groundskeeper had resided. However, now that the grounds more or less kept themselves, the path was rather overgrown. Underbrush had proliferated under the canopy of tall old trees where twilight gloom was beginning to deepen. The cottage was, the last time I had seen it, in an advanced state of dilapidation. Approaching it, I saw half the roof had fallen in. Then I smelled burning wood, saw smoke rising from the chimney and a bright glow shining from the open door. A squatter! We had had trouble with them before. Outraged at violation of our property by this uninvited stranger, I ran to the door and burst in.

A tousle-headed man was crouching by the fireplace, twirling a spit on which a rabbit carcass was roasting. He leaped to his feet upon my entrance, surprise writ large on his bearded face. Just as quickly he whirled to rescue his rabbit from imminent disaster on the glowing embers.

"You're trespassing! What are you doing here? Who are you?" I screeched.

"Wasn't posted," he shot back

"It surely is. You didn't see the sign or you ignored it. And where did you shoot that rabbit? That sign also says NO HUNTING."

"Didn't hunt. Got this rabbit in a field a mile or more away, didn't shoot him, snared him. Seems you're bent out of shape all out of proportion to my trespass. I'm not dangerous at all, mild-mannered and soft-spoken is how folks usually describe me."

Fine white teeth flashed in the grin that parted his hairy face. His voice was well modulated, diction excellent, pleasant. My hasty anger was fading a bit.

"You can finish your supper and stay the night in shelter, but I want you gone first thing in the morning. I'm calling Deputy Bigelow and he'll be around to see you are gone." I was beginning to find his polite responses and agreeable tone disarming.

"Is that Jud Bigelow?"

"Well, yes, I think his first name is Judson."

"When you call him, tell him it's Teddy Boy hanging out in this shack. He'll be glad to hear from me. We grew up together over in Perry County."

"I want your full, proper name. I'm not going to give him some juvenile nickname. What is it?" I asked

"Theodore Roosevelt Vance, ma'am. And you?"

Taken by surprise, I answered, "I'm Clio DeVille…"

He was prodding his nicely browned rabbit as he interrupted me,

“This fellow seems to be done to a turn. Want to share a leg with me, he’s a big one, plenty for two.

“I certainly do not. Where are you going to sleep? Rain is forecast for tonight and this roof is not likely to keep it out.”

“There’s roof enough over the back room. I’ll just spread my bed roll there and sleep snug. Thanks for your concern.”

By now, I had seen he wasn’t ragged and his clothes were clean. If he was a hobo, he was a cut above the usual tramp knocking on the door of Hauteville House. I turned, calling out from the door,

“And make sure that fire is completely out when you leave!”

Then I hurried out of the cabin and home along the path to the house. It was now full dark and I was wondering if I had made a mistake in allowing this rather engaging stranger to stay the night on the property.

§ Four §

Mrs. Ryan met me at the door, wringing her hands. "Evelyn just called and Walter won't be coming. He fell out of the hay loft and is in the hospital. Broken leg. Now what do we do?"

Walter Stark was a young fellow just getting started on a one-horse farm down the road, with a wife and four kids, and taking night watches to earn a much needed supplement to his income. My first reaction was irritation—how inconsiderate of him, what did he mean, falling out of his loft and causing trouble for us, now Mrs. Bettle and I would have to double up, damn it all.... Then I remembered good manners and civility commanded compassion—Walter, poor guy, wouldn't be able to work the farm all summer, much less sit with Papa; Evelyn and the kids were doomed to short rations....

"We'll get right on a replacement first thing in the morning. I'll wash up and change clothes now. Tell Mrs. Bettle I'll be along in just a few minutes."

I changed into shirt and jeans and slippers. I told Mrs. Bettle to get a good night's sleep and be ready at 8 A.M. to relieve me. Papa was asleep and didn't wake when I came in. I took up my post and devoted my musings to planning the next day's search for a night sitter. About 3 A.M., I was dozing when the sounds of Papa choking and gargling brought me wide awake. His eyes were closed, his mouth gaping, body arched, only head and heels touching the bed, arms flailing at his sides. Hastily I grabbed the syringe and vial of medicine from the bedside stand, pulled the sheathe off the needle, loaded the syringe, and injected its contents into the wasted muscle of Papa's right arm. He writhed for another two or three minutes before he went limp. The seizure was over. I straightened the bedclothes and held his sippy cup to his lips; he was always thirsty after a seizure. Another few minutes and the habitual rigidity of his body returned and his breathing came slow and deep. I relaxed again in the chair and the rest of the night passed uneventfully.

Mrs. Bettle came in on the dot of eight; her sturdy body swathed in crisp white, her rosy face set in an expression of calm resignation. I nodded a groggy greeting and went down to breakfast, but before I ate I called Deputy Bigelow. He was disposed to be chatty, as I was not.

"Sure, I'll get right over there, the old groundskeeper's cottage, you say? Teddy Boy, the guy said? Wow, it's been a while since I've seen him. Maybe 20 years. We used to have some good times together when we were kids. I suppose you heard Walt Stark's bad luck? Evelyn's mom is gonna tend the kids while she goes back to work at the diner. Oh, and how's Mr. DeVille these days? Do you know yet what you're gonna do for a night nurse? I'll ask around today and let ya know what I come up with."

His good bye was cheerier than mine. I needed at least two cups of coffee before I could be pleasant over the phone, even more before I could face hunting up Walter's replacement. I was in better temper when Pierce came in to tell me the deputy was out front to see me. I went out to find "Teddy Boy" in the passenger seat of the patrol car and Bigelow leaning on the right side door. The two of them grinned at me and Bigelow straightened and waved a casual hand at his passenger.

"Yep, there he was, right where you said. Came peacefully just like I knew he would. Ha, Ha. Speak up, Teddy, tell the nice lady what you're really up to."

Theodore Roosevelt Vance unfolded his long, lanky frame from the seat of the car and emerged bending in a bow worthy of Buckingham Palace.

"Miss DeVille," he said. "I trust this lovely morning finds you in good health and good temper. I spent a thoroughly comfortable and restful night under your hospitable roof, what there was of it."

"Humph!" I snorted. The deputy spoke up,

"Hey, now that Walt is out of commission, what about a replacement? I can recommend Ted here. He's free, needs a job, whaddya say?"

"Well, Deputy, I can't take on any hobo that comes along, even if he comes with your recommendation. I have to know some background on anyone who comes into this house and undertakes a responsible position. I plan to ask Reverend McLinn to suggest a local man with good references."

"Oh, Ted can furnish references, he was born and raised around here. Even Rev McLinn knows him or did before he became a world traveler. Speak up, Ted, tell Ms. DeVille where you been and what you been doin'."

"OK, I'll begin with graduation from Perry High School the same year as Jud. Went to MIT and got an engineering degree, joined the Peace Corps, spent assignments in Kenya and Greece, got married to and divorced from an English lady who didn't much like living in Northern India while I was building dams there, taught in a boys' school in Thailand for a couple of years, inherited enough money to let me travel in hiking boots with knapsack and alpenstock through the former Soviet Union, and to start on a book describing my adventures."

He paused for breath and Deputy Bigelow burst out, "What's Alpenstock? Some kind of European beer?"

"An ironshod walking staff, you numskull. My family is all scattered now but lately I had a hankering to come back here where I grew up. Thought the atmosphere would be good for finishing the book, cheaper to live around here than in a big city, and peaceful. But I do need a job, since my travels have been pretty hard on my capital. I'd work for room and board and $10 a week."

"Would you work seven nights a week? Watching a sick man

for eight hours, no breaks, ready to administer medication on short notice? We could make it $20 a week and room and board."

"Yeah, I reckon. That would give me daytimes to work on my book. Are you offering me the job, ma'am?"

"Not yet. I meant it when I said I had to have references. I'll talk to Reverend McLinn and I want telephone numbers for your Peace Corps supervisors and the school in Thailand. I'll let you know. In the meantime, keep Deputy Bigelow informed of your whereabouts."

"No prob, Ms. DeVille," the deputy said. "I'm taking him home with me. Sara Jane won't mind an old pal in the spare room and at the table for a few days. You can call her or me when you make up your mind."

§ Five §

A week later, Mrs. Bettle and I were both exhausted; continual shift changing had led to enough sleep deprivation to fray both our good natures. So, when telephoned recommendations from Reverend McLinn and the Peace Corps supervisors and a letter promised by the Thai schoolmaster arrived and were adequate to hire Ted (as he asked to be called), everyone was grateful. Ted learned in 20 minutes to recognize symptoms and to master injection technique. Mrs. Bettle and I gave one another 8-hour sleeps before going back to our 4-on-4-off daytime schedule. Mrs. Ryan prepared a room for Ted in the east wing where she and Pierce slept, and he joined the four of us at meals at the long table in the servants hall. He had tied his long hair up in a neat pony tail and now shaved daily, disclosing regular facial features and sparkling brown eyes. The two local girls that Mrs. Ryan hired to come in for cleaning three days a week promptly fell in love with him and lunch times turned into social occasions of considerable jollity. Ted had an inexhaustible fund of personal adventure stories and descriptions of exotic locales and related them amusingly whenever encouraged to do so. He often wandered in as I worked in the library—to borrow a book or check something in the big dictionary or simply to exchange a pleasant but brief comment on the weather. I found myself enjoying him and congratulating myself for having the good fortune to hire him.

In some ways Ted was a breath of fresh air in the dusty, musty ambience of the small closed-in society of Hauteville House. In other ways he was a trouble maker. Unwittingly, entirely innocently, he brought disturbing new influences to bear on our lives, chiefly, I must admit, on mine. He spoke of far places, foreign ideas, unfamiliar customs, strange occupations. Pierce and Mrs. Ryan found them entertaining, I found them upsetting. While I was poking around in dry volumes of ancient writings and the ideas of long gone statesmen and philosophers—he had walked among the ruins where those sages had walked. While I was probing the meanings and permutations of the words they had left behind. he had smelled the smells of those fetid bazaars where once they shopped for their groceries. My life was as empty of color and life as the pages I turned and words I typed into manuscript.

Ted sat with Papa all night in a great silence marked by an occasional flurry of excitement, then spent the daytime writing and recalling his exciting adventures and the exotic places he had visited. His life had been part of the modern world He had flown in airplanes, ridden on trains, sat in movie theatres, gone to pizza parlors. I sat with Papa for long dreary hours, and went on to spend more long dreary hours poring over books and shuffling papers in an occupation with neither purpose nor profit. Trips to the village to buy toothpaste or cough drops or stamps, to have my teeth cleaned or.... Oh, Hell! I was alive but not living, I had to admit it. Hate rose up in my throat like bitter bile whenever I let my thoughts roam in that direction.

And then, as Ted grew more integrated into our lives and his brief visits to the library grew into real conversations, he asked questions. Why this? Why that? I was appalled as I realized that I had no credible answers. Why didn't we have more watchers for Papa? Why was I spending half my life under a burden that could be bought and paid for? I could only say lamely that I had never asked Papa's lawyer, a man named Horace Elder, for more help, that I hadn't seen him in this house more than once a year in all the years that Papa had lain helpless and speechless. And most damning of all, that I hadn't thought his indifference odd. I began to realize that I had failed to take control of what little life I had, and that perhaps it wouldn't be impossible to exert myself to do so.

One day, Ted's question was even more personal.

"Why don't you get a more becoming haircut? You'd be a stunner with that dark, dark hair and blue, blue eyes. And if you got more sleep and outdoor exercise, those dark circles under your eyes would go away. You've got a pretty good figure, why don't you ditch those smocky Mother Hubbards you wear so often and invest in knit shirts and tailored slacks? Colorful T-shirts and sweat shirts would be attractive and practical additions to your wardrobe. "

My first reaction was indignation. "How I look and what I wear is none of your business. You've got a smart mouth!"

Ted grinned and shrugged and left the room. Without a target for my anger, I began to have second thoughts. It was true that spending fewer hours at Papa's bedside would get me more sleep and outdoor exercise, or let me go more often to the village beauty parlor to have my hair styled and trimmed or to the shops to freshen or enlarge my wardrobe. I pushed aside the manuscript at hand and rose to pace up and down. Pacing, I alternately fumed at Ted's impertinence and pondered possibilities.

Then Pierce came in to say "He's expecting you, Miss Clio."

And I replied politely, "Thank you, Pierce, I'll be right up." Going up the stairs, I ruminated on Pierce's manner of reminding me of the time; the mindset of this old servant saw my shift on watch as a duty I was expected to fulfill. Fleetingly, I wondered just where my duty began and ended, and then I met Mrs. Bettle coming out of his door.

"I've just given him his medication, Miss Clio; he ought to be asleep very soon," she said.

"Thank you, Mrs. Bettle," I replied and entered his room.

§ Six §

THAT AFTERNOON I mulled over some of the ideas Ted had stirred up during the morning. The watch was uneventful. There had been no seizure, the indwelling catheter didn't plug up, and thank goodness, Mrs. Bettle had taken care of changing the bed linens and the diaper. Papa didn't open his eyes once during the four hours I sat there. When Mrs. Bettle came back for the next shift, I got up rather stiffly and made my escape into the afternoon sunshine. The hot weather had broken in a summer thunderstorm which had refreshed the air and laid the dust. I walked down to the road and collected the mail, such as it was: three Occupants and a letter for Mrs. Ryan from her son in Florida. More evidence of my life out of the mainstream—I couldn't remember when a letter addressed to me personally had arrived. By the time I got back to the house, I had decided on two rather drastic steps, drastic for me, that is. I packaged up a spare copy of my manuscript translations of three Greek comedies, planning to go to the village tomorrow to dispatch it to Marcus Atwater. Atwater had once been a fairly frequent correspondent of Papa's; he was a classical scholar himself, as well as a publisher of esoterica. I asked in the enclosed letter for his opinion of the quality of the translation and an estimate of the publishability of these modern English versions. Then, I called the village salon—*Elegance* was the name written in flowing gold script on the window of the storefront where Sally Vernon presided over a barber chair and a washstand—to make an appointment for a hair cut. I might as well make one trip serve two purposes.

The second drastic step was a letter to Horace Elder at Elder-Thackeray, the law firm that handled DeVille affairs, informing Elder I wanted him to call on me at the House within the week to discuss some changes in the nursing arrangements. I rewrote .that letter three times before I thought it displayed the right degree of firmness and businesslike tone. In all of my previous contacts with Mr. Elder, his condescension had just barely stopped short of an avuncular pat on the head, but I was determined this time to take charge of the conversation.

I changed my mind twice before dinner, not about the haircut, but about posting the letter to Elder and the package to Atwater. Was I being too daring? What if Atwater panned my texts? Called them worthless, puerile? What if Elder found my feeble attempts at self-assertion merely humorous? Or attempted to browbeat me into some form of submissive acceptance of his decisions? In our past encounters, I had found Elder distant and condescending, turning away my diffident inquiries with platitudes or a retreat into smiling silence. Finally, I told myself to stop thinking about what might happen; I would cast the die, come what may.

Dinner that night was even jollier than usual. Ted regaled us with the story of his brush with a Swiss guard at the Vatican and a near escape from incarceration in the papal poky. His mocking mimicry of the guard's heavy Teutonic accent and his derisive description of the guard's nether garments fell short of respect for papal dignity but he got away with it. Mrs. Bettle was the only Catholic in the household and she was on watch duty at the time; both Pierce and Mrs. Ryan were born and bred Anglican and always ready for putdowns on Romans. As we rose from the table, Ted took me aside and said,

"I didn't intend to offend you this morning. You were quite right, it's none of my business what you do or how you do it. It's just that

I hate waste and I do think your life is being wasted. I won't bring it up again. Friends?"

I nodded and shook the hand he extended. Tears stung my eyes briefly and I swallowed hard before I went back for a little more work in the library before my evening watching stint.

§ Seven §

I FOLLOWED THROUGH WITH the haircut, asking Sally for something short, easy to care for, reasonably stylish. She turned me out with what was called, in my childhood, a "pixie." It was surprisingly flattering and my table mates commented approvingly. Buoyed up by their approval, I was expectant of early answers from Atwater and Elder. My optimism was deflated by a phone call from Mr. Elder's secretary informing me he was out of the country for another two weeks but would be in touch upon his return. The only word I had from Mr. Atwater was the little green slip from the post office certifying delivery of my package. The next two weeks dragged by in unrelieved dreary routine until one day Pierce came into the library, a flash of excitement sparkling in his eyes.

"Mr. Horace Elder on the hall telephone for you, Miss Clio."

I almost laughed; he specified the hall telephone as if it were only one of a dozen scattered throughout the house. There had never been but one in the house in my lifetime, but Pierce was a survivor from a more formal and sumptuous time and ceremony was as engrained in his manners as was the blood that pumped through his body.

"Thank you, Pierce."

To please Pierce, I walked ceremoniously to the telephone stand beside the stair and took up the handset, nodding dismissal to Pierce.

"This is Clio DeVille."

"Ah, yes, Miss Clio, Horace Elder here." His voice was as unctuous as I recalled it from the last time I had heard it. "I regret my delayed response to your message, I trust my secretary explained I was out of the country. I hope all is well at Hauteville House."

"Thank you for your reply, Mr. Elder. There has been no change at Hauteville House; Mr. Armand is much as always. I, however, would like for you to stop by for a talk with me about changing some of the current arrangements."

"My dear, I will be only too happy to talk over any problems you have and at any length, but may we not do it by phone? Stopping by is somewhat inconvenient; it's some 45 minutes from my office in the city to Hauteville House. "

He made it sound like the distance from the earth to the moon, but I held my ground. I wanted him to come here, to be here, to see how Papa had to be cared for. I kept my voice cool and businesslike.

"I am extending an invitation to lunch here at the House, any day at your convenience, shall we say 11:30?"

He apparently sensed my resolve. "Just let me have my girl check my calendar. A moment, please. I have an incoming call, may I put you on hold?"

Neat put down, I thought. "Of course, I'll be waiting." Such a busy man!

His girl was back on the phone quite soon, proposing next Friday if that would be satisfactory, apologizing that Mr. Elder's call was going to take a lot longer, and should he call back?

"No," I said, "he needn't. We can pick up our conversation on Friday."

This guy was good, knew all the tricks to put me on the defensive. I would be obliged to remain steadfast in my determination to control our face-to-face encounter.

Friday, I was looking out a library window when, on the dot of 11:30, a smartly uniformed chauffeur drew up Elder's long black limousine in the drive and leaped out to open its door. Elder emerged deliberately and stood for a moment as if surveying the prospective battlefield. Then he waved the driver off to a parking place to wait and strutted to the front door. He made quite a figure, a short burly body garbed in what was obviously an expensively tailored suit, topped by a ruddy face under carefully barbered white locks. Pierce opened the door before Elder could lift the heavy lion's head knocker and ceremoniously ushered him in, took his hat, showed him to a chair in the drawing room (dust sheets having been removed for the occasion), and again ceremoniously, came to notify me in the library that my guest had arrived.

I limited one-up manship to just three minutes before I went to greet Mr. Elder. After we had shaken hands and he had declined a sherry, we repaired to the dining room where Pierce had laid the small table in the bay with its view of the green but unkempt terrace and parterre. We bandied trivialities over Mrs. Ryan's *cordon bleu* quiche accompanied by spinach and mushroom salad (raspberry vinaigrette dressing), but I got down to business over pineapple cream mousse and coffee.

"I regret your having to travel so far to meet with me, but I hoped you would be more amenable to my inquiries and requests after you had visited Papa's bedside, because it's Papa's situation which most concerns me."

Elder peered under his bushy white brows, then took a forkful of mousse and a sip of coffee as he replied.

"Ah, and has Armand's condition worsened lately? I was under the impression he was much the same and his care had become rather routine."

"Well, yes, it's the routine we need to reconsider. When we finish lunch, I hope to show you upstairs to his room so you can see for yourself."

Elder finished his mousse and coffee in a leisurely fashion, folded his napkin neatly, patted his bulging vest, and rose graciously to pull back my chair, but Pierce beat him to it. So far, I imagined I was ahead of the game, on to the next set.

§ Eight §

As I had hoped, Mrs. Bettle had just emptied the urine collection bag and completed the change of linens and Papa's diaper. I could see Elder's nose twitch in response to the somewhat aromatic atmosphere of the room, but he kept his composure and greeted Mrs. Bettle politely. Papa's lids did not even flicker as Elder stood over the bed and addressed him amiably.

"Ah, well, Armand. I see you are faring about as well as can be expected, getting good care, and staying well. Not too many seizures, I trust, but quick relief when they occur. I talked with Dr. Eisenstein before coming to visit and he reassured me that matters were being handled well by Clio and your nurses. I am giving the DeVille affairs my usual attention and you may set your mind at rest about them."

Papa's eyelids fell closed, his only reaction to our presence, and stayed closed.

"Is he asleep?" Elder whispered.

"Perhaps. It's hard to tell," I replied aloud. "Let's go out to the sitting room to continue our conversation."

The sitting room of the master suite had been especially cleaned when the dust covers had been removed; the drapes had been opened, and Armand I's rather shabby divan, armchairs, and carpet appeared in all their faded Victorian glory. We sat down and before Elder could begin to pontificate, I started in,

"Now, Mr. Elder, I consider the most pressing concern in Papa's care to be the personal distress it causes us, his caregivers. Currently we have a young man sitting with him from midnight to eight A.M. seven nights a week, but we do not expect him to remain with us indefinitely. Mrs. Bettle and I take turns in four-hour shifts to cover sixteen hours every day, and have done so for the past five years. On those rare occasions when neither she nor I can cover more than one shift, we engage an off-duty nurse from the Home Care Service. We find, however, the Service staff is overbooked and reluctant to be responsible for handling Papa's special needs. Both Mrs. Bettle and I are nearly worn out with watching. As I see it, the solution to the problem is to engage one or even two more live-in nurses or medically competent aides to provide coverage. All of us could then have relief from the now-continuous responsibilities."

It was a long speech. I had rehearsed my spiel and thought I had got it out quite expeditiously. At least Elder hadn't drowsed as I made my pitch. However, he did take his time to reply, massaging his chin and squinching up his eyes as he pondered. I waited patiently. At last, he spoke,

"Now, Clio, I can see how your duties might drain your patience and energy. Nevertheless, in my estimation watching Armand cannot be particularly physically demanding. You have these strong young men to lift him and Pierce who is both valet and butler to groom him. He is not always seizing and surely you and the other watchers can read or sleep or at least doze on your shifts…."

I broke in, "One cannot read at the light level the doctor prescribes for the room. As for lifting him, more often than not, handling his body for massages, diapering, and changing night shirts and bed linens falls to me or Mrs. Bettle. Sleeping is out of the question, dozing is unwise. The watcher occupies a straight chair on doctor's orders to inhibit dozing and to allow instant reaction to the start of a seizure. Furthermore, a shift rarely passes without at least one seizure. What is becoming intolerable is the continual demand on me and Mrs. Bettle to spend eight hours of every day of our lives on the *qui vive*, in a gloomy, closed up room, deprived of adequate exercise and pleasant distractions.

The drain on our physical and psychic energy grows greater every day. Mrs. Bettle speaks often of leaving her position and her home in this house and going to live with her son in Florida. Losing her services would be disastrous."

Another long speech, this one unrehearsed and verging on passionate. The man didn't want to empathize in the least little way! After more chin rubbing and squinting, he replied.

"Clio, I must inform you that your father's financial affairs, despite my close and careful attention, have prospered less well in recent years. You will have noticed that we have retreated on the upkeep of Hauteville House and Mrs. Ryan and Pierce have been cautioned to be frugal with household expenses. I can perhaps authorize adding one care-giver to your staff, not a nurse—the salary would be out of line with available funds—but a medically trained aide could be considered…."

I interrupted again, "Are you saying we can't *afford* help? I've not heard in my entire life in this house that we were short of money. I assumed the grounds had been neglected because staff to tend them was unnecessary in the absence of use by the family. Mrs. Ryan and Pierce have never breathed a word about watching expenses. My last tutor left the house saying his new job was with 'another millionaire' and that was only 20 years ago. Why has this dearth of means been kept from me? I'm not a minor and in Papa's incapacity—even though you hold his power of attorney and can act for him in every way—I certainly have a right to know when our financial status is severely impaired."

My voice had risen to a dangerous pitch and Mrs. Bettle had come to check that the door to the bedroom was shut firmly. Loud sounds sometimes set Papa off. I sincerely hoped she had not heard any of the preceding conversation.

Elder's face had flushed on hearing my tirade.

"Clio, I very much hope you are not imputing dereliction of my duty to you and your father. For the last 15 years I have bent my every effort to the faithful execution of your father's wishes, regardless of personal inconvenience. I have in all things lived up to Armand's confidence in my integrity. I find it painful to muster a defense of my management of his affairs to you now, but I am willing to explain. The capital holdings in trust have not decreased but the income they generate has. The recession has hit the stock market hard and the assets that provide the DeVille income have not been providing as generously as they have in the past. Perhaps I should have informed you but I preferred to spare you the worry. I regret I must tell you hard truths now and I hope you will accept them calmly. Your life style is in no immediate danger of major change but prudence must be exercised in managing it. I will authorize another salaried position in the household at pay equal to 60% of Mrs. Bettle's and you may start negotiations to engage a nurse's aide. I suggest a live-in rather than a non-resident employee as a less expensive addition. That is the best I can do to relieve your concerns. I consider the subject closed."

He rose from his seat, the stony expression on his face making it clear he had no more to say and wanted to hear no more from me. I rang the bell for Pierce to show him out and saw him go without a word of farewell. Mentally, I added him to my list of hates. Then I went to my bedroom, shoved my face in my pillow and cried it soggy.

§ Nine §

My tears were compounded of frustration and anger. I had been not only living a sterile existence, I had done so without knowing why. And now that I knew why, I was seemingly helpless to do anything about it. Not only helpless to act myself, but literally without help since the family lawyer had little sympathy for me or for the problems of Hauteville House. I got up, mopped my red eyes dry, combed my hair, and went to take up my shift at Papa's bedside. As I passed Mrs. Bettle in the doorway, I counted on the gloom of the room to hide the signs of tears.

My musings today zeroed in on Elder's hasty insistence on his integrity and his abrupt termination of further discussion. Didn't self justification bulk large in his answers? Was he afraid to let me delve into the DeVille financial situation? Could the shortfall of the DeVille income possibly be due to Elder's mismanagement of the capital? Or worse, his diversion of income from it? Power of attorney on behalf of a man totally incapable of understanding how the power was being used was power indeed. And because I took no interest in family business affairs after Papa's finally complete incapability, Elder had become a free agent, no longer accountable to a DeVille. Not only could I not remember ever having seen reports or audits from his office, I could not remember ever *expecting* to see any. I had never thought to question the arrangement. I was becoming aware of deep, burning resentment against Papa's thoughtlessness as he arranged the future of DeVille finances without involving me.

At the end of my shift, I accosted Pierce and asked him if

he knew of papers addressed to Papa from Elder's office. He said, yes, a fat, official-looking manila envelope came from Elder-Thackeray once a year. He used to give it to Papa who would open it, glance through the contents, and then instruct him to file it in a cabinet in the library. But eventually Papa, retreating into catatonia, just waved it aside and Pierce filed it unopened and unread. Lately, Pierce simply filed the envelope without even showing it to Papa. As for other papers, Mrs. Ryan had for years submitted quarterly reports detailing household expenditures for Elder's review. Someone in his office vetted the accounting, sometimes added comment or instructions, initialed it, and returned it for filing. Mrs. Ryan and Pierce routinely checked those documents together before filing them.

I went to the library and searched for a filing cabinet. Finding it, I saw it was stuffed with papers, the quarterly statements carefully arranged chronologically, the yearly envelopes as well. According to the postmarks, the last opened envelope from Elder-Thackeray had been filed some six years ago. I pushed aside the current translation materials on my work table and started to open the oldest sealed envelope. I was promptly in over my head; I couldn't make heads or tails of the close-printed lists of securities—bonds and share holdings, I presumed. I did recognize tax forms although their complexities escaped me. I turned on the desk lamp and started to shuffle through the papers but when I realized I had opened a Pandora's box, feeble tears began to flow and I put my head down on my folded arms in utter discouragement.

"Hey, lady, what's the trouble? Did that fat cat lawyer with his fancy wheels give you a hard time? Here, this is a perfectly clean handkerchief, without which as a gentleman *sans peur et sans reproche* I am never to be found. Will that help?"

I lifted up my head and reached gratefully for Ted's handkerchief, which was actually a man-size double-thickness Kleenex. In the meantime, he hiked one hip up on the corner of the table. Sitting there, he caught a glimpse of the heading on the tax forms and said,

"Well, if that's your income tax you're figuring, I can see why you are crying."

I was just devastated enough by the day's events that I lost all reticence and spilled the DeVille beans: what Elder had told me; what I had got from him in the way of help; what doubts and fears had surfaced; my panic in the face of all these papers. Ted listened quietly and ever practical, said,

"Let's begin by thanking our lucky stars you got a nurse's aide out of him. That's a big help. The next thing you or Mrs. Ryan should do is get busy hunting up someone to fill the position. You could put up an ad in the village stores or Post Office. Or you might consider one of those girls who comes to clean. Roseanne is the smarter and more mature of the two; it would be as easy to teach her to cope with a seizure as it was for you to teach me. Mrs. Ryan can always find another local girl to do cleaning."

"But how am I going to figure out what's in these papers?" I wailed. "I'll have to understand what they're all about if I'm to investigate what's gone on in the last five years or so."

"I've got a friend down in the village, went to school with him. His name is Bonelle Harvill and he's a CPA. Ask him to help you wade through this stuff. He's like a priest, what he hears and sees he keeps confidential."

"But I'd have to pay him. Where would I get the money without Elder knowing what I was up to? I can't get it out of household petty cash and Mrs. Ryan can't put in for a check without explaining the purpose."

"Explain the situation to Bonelle and ask him to take the job on spec."

"What's 'on spec'?"

"You'll pay him when you get things settled. He's a pretty good egg and I think he will probably go for a deal like that. There's a lot of curiosity in the village about Hauteville House and the doings up here. He might even take you on just for the heck of it. Wait a minute, I'll get his number."

He went out to the hall to bring back the phone book and read me Harvill's number. I wrote it down on the Pandora's box envelope. Bless Ted's heart, I now had something positive to do tomorrow. Tell Mrs. Bettle about the new help, get Mrs. Ryan started on hiring a nurse's aide, and call Mr. Harvill to come over for a chat.

§ Ten §

Mr. Harvill was on the doorstep the following afternoon, having arrived in a daffodil yellow VW with a plastic daisy bobbing on the radio antenna. Harvill himself was elfin, short, plump, topped off with a brush of flaming red hair over a pair of piercing grey eyes. A quietly reassuring manner and an open, smiling countenance recommended him to me immediately and I faced him comfortably across the big desk in the library. I had decided, since Ted had told me I could depend on confidentiality, to tell him everything—from the details of Papa's total debility to my fears for Elder's honesty. He listened intently, occasionally asking a question to clarify a statement, nodding from time to time. I wound up my story with a question for him,

"If you were to help me out with this mess of paper, when would you expect to be paid for your time?"

"First, let me warn you that your mistrust may be misplaced or unwarranted, there may be no malfeasance, your lawyer may be guilty of nothing or guilty only of poor judgment. Looking into this situation may be opening a can of worms without a fishing hole to dabble in. On the other hand, the can of worms may turn into an expensive legal battle that you may not be psychologically prepared to conduct. Have you thought this through?"

"No, but I'm convinced that the points you make are perfectly valid and I *am* prepared to explore possibilities. I'm convinced that whatever I learn now will be valuable in the future; the day will come when Papa dies and I will be forced to deal with matters arising from his death. If I find Elder's skirts are clean, so be it.

Perhaps I can dismiss him and engage someone more empathetic to manage the DeVille financial affairs. If Elder turns out to be guilty of something, I can decide what to do when I find out what the something is and how it might be remedied. Is that an answer for you?"

"That was a pretty good answer, I'd say. So my answer to your question about pay is this: I'll audit your financial documents on a handshake and a one dollar retainer. When or if I find circumstances justify my billing you, we'll talk about it then. What do you say to that?"

"Sounds just like Perry Mason. I'm assuming the dollar buys me confidentiality."

"For everything that's legal, it does."

I got up and went round the desk to shake his hand. I felt like hugging him, I was so taken with his easy charm and so grateful for his common sense approach, but concluded that was pushing the envelope. I thought I was perhaps becoming too susceptible to kind words from new male acquaintances.

"By the way," he said, "you can call me Bonny, all my friends do."

Maybe it wasn't too soon to count on a friendly connection. We finished our conversation by making arrangements to meet regularly to organize and transfer documents. I rounded up four shiny quarters from the desk drawer and he wrote out a receipt. When I gestured helplessly at the hapless pile of stuff from the six-year old envelope on my work table, he offered to put the contents in order and spend an hour or so looking through them to get an idea of their nature.

Just then Mrs. Ryan appeared at the library door, saying she was interviewing Roseanne for the nurse's aide job and would like me to sit in. I excused myself and went with her. The first thing I learned was that Roseanne's surname was Leonard, the second thing that she was no pushover. It was a blessing that we did not have to explain Papa's problem; she had witnessed almost all the worst features of his sick bed during her work in the room.

She told us she thought the wage Mrs. Ryan was offering was too low for such responsible work. Since Mrs. Ryan had started bargaining at 50% of Mrs. Bettle's salary, negotiations to increase the amount were soon successful at 55%, Saturdays half day only, Sundays off. Mrs. Ryan wasn't a pushover either, but she did have to promise a raise after six months of satisfactory performance. As it happened, Roseanne's younger sister, Lily, wanted daily work and would be glad to take over Roseanne's cleaning tasks. Mrs. Bettle had already given her approval of Roseanne and said she and Roseanne would work out a schedule that relieved both her and me. Roseanne and Lily would start their new jobs Monday next, after Roseanne had been trained to perform bedside chores to Mrs. Bettle's standards. I didn't yet know how much free time I would gain or the pattern it would have, but whatever—I was looking forward to the relief, and so was Mrs. Bettle.

§ ELEVEN §

THE SCHEDULE WORKED out Monday through Friday with Roseanne on 8-11:30 A.M. and 1-5 P.M.; Mrs. Bettle or me 11:30 A.M. to 1:30 P.M.; Roseanne 8-12 every Saturday morning, and Mrs. Bettle and I dividing evenings and the remaining weekend hours. Having so much free time was wonderful for both of us. I spent some of it walking the woods, although the coming of fall weather curtailed my outdoor time to some extent. I also set up a weekly appointment for hair care at Sally Vernon's *Elegance*, and spent the rest of the afternoon window shopping and buying additions to my wardrobe. Mrs. Bettle started knitting an afghan and indulged in jigsaw puzzles and gossip with Mrs. Ryan and Pierce (the three of them favored the same soap operas and the tribulations and triumphs of the characters provided endless topics for discussion).

I still had not heard from Marcus Atwater but I didn't fret. I was engrossed in new work on a translation of some of Ovid's spicier tales. I had a notion in the back of my mind that the lively stuff framed in modern English might appeal to contemporary readers. If I could come up with something both publishable and saleable, I might have a source of a modest but independent income. My optimism was obliged to be guarded but there was always a chance. I was also buying a $1.00 lottery ticket every time I had my hair done. Lightning does strike, even though very rarely, and more than one lightning rod doubles opportunities for a hit, even when the odds are quoted at thirty million to one.

Ted was jubilant over the progress he was making on his book.

He explained his work program, saying that during the night watch he planned his next chapter in his mind and the next morning after breakfast he sat down to put out a couple thousand words before sleeping. When he waked in the afternoon, he revised, rewrote—and sometimes trashed—his morning text. He had sent three trial chapters off to a publisher of travel books, a man who had already bought some magazine articles from him. The feedback had been enthusiastic and Ted said, if the enthusiasm held up, a finished book, contract, and advance would be forthcoming in December. He warned us, he would probably be moving on when he had "dough in hand." He had in mind roaming Central America for a follow up book. All of us had nothing but best wishes for his writing career and further books but we dreaded losing him. For the time being, we put off thoughts of the need for another night watcher, although we did make discreet inquiries as to the progress of Walter Stark's broken leg.

Mr. Harvill (I was finding it difficult to call him "Bonny") came around every Monday and Wednesday afternoon. Pierce and Ted rummaged storage to find a sturdy table to set up for him in the library .His first move was to empty the filing cabinet and identify its oldest contents; he said he needed to study Papa's approach to financial issues prior to his withdrawal from involvement in them. In the process of sorting and organizing the old documents, he found the trust instrument Papa had drawn up when I was in my teens and the doctors had first told him of his impending disability. The trustee was the First National Bank of Columbus and the listing of assets assigned to the trust encompassed stocks and bonds that at the time the trust was established were worth almost three million dollars. Bonny said he would have to study their histories in the intervening years in order to identify changes in the portfolio and to estimate current value. The trustee's accounting initially came directly to Papa, but after Elder assumed Papa's power of attorney, went to Elder. Elder, who also administered a portfolio of securities not included in the trust, then incorporated the trustee's accounting into his periodic reports to Papa. His reports also contained a meticulous record of cash disbursements for taxes, household expenses, building maintenance, and such.

"It will be slow work," Bonny said, looking up from the stacks of paper with his engaging smile, "but a thorough audit always is. What I've seen so far leads me to think your father was once a canny investor and a careful manager of his resources."

"I remember Papa as a brilliant scholar and he could very well have been a financial wizard besides. However, that was a side of him I never experienced. Looking back on our personal relationship, I see the vast distance that separated us, despite the closeness we shared in our translation work. Never did I take notice nor inquire into his decision to put control of our finances, and more—control of our lives—completely into Elder's hands. I had not even known of the regular reports Elder provided to him. I simply assumed whatever Papa did was the right thing to do. I guess I'm the original example of head-in-the-sand existence."

I made my rueful confession in a tearful voice.

"Don't take it so hard," Bonny soothed. "Most only children see their parents or, in your case parent, as omnipotent and omniscient, possessed of perfect judgment and always acting from the best of intentions. The habit of trusting parents formed when you are very young is hard to break, especially if you grow up and stay under the same roof year after year, even more so in the absence of outside influence or criticism. According to the gossip I've heard in the village, your entire life has been spent inside these walls—a private education by resident governesses and tutors, and a seamless transition from that childhood to the role of colleague to your father in his absorption with the classics. One of my sources related in horrified tones that you were never allowed to join the Girl Scouts or to go to camp. I guess there must be a lot of unsold cookies out there."

I chuckled, then queried, "What makes you so wise, Bonny?"

"I majored in child psychology before I learned I'd make a better living from accounting. My psychology education didn't make me wise, it just made me thoughtful and very tolerant of human foibles."

He grinned and turned over another stack of papers. I grinned back, he was a really nice guy. I congratulated myself on his assistance. Maybe opening Pandora's box wasn't going to be the devastating process I feared.

§ Twelve §

THE SNOWS BEGAN in the first week of December. Ted had to go to New York on business with his book and during the week he was away, Walter Stark came back on the night watch. He fitted his tractor with a blade and plowed out the estate roads as he came and went for his shift. Bonny Harvill kept to his schedule of visits by putting up his VW in favor of a Jeep with four-wheel drive. Roseanne, bundled up in scarves and mittens and shod in boots and heavy socks, came to work over the fields and through the wood, arriving with her cheeks as rosy as her name. My outdoor exercise consisted of shoveling the front drive and walks once or twice a day. The grocery man grumbled at the weather but nevertheless managed to make his deliveries regularly so we fared quite as well as in the summer.

I was making great headway with my translations of Ovid, and Bonny had whittled down the mass of old documents to two categories: one a selection of those prior to the past five years and another, those of the last five years. On each visit, he brought along a black bag containing his electronic calculator and laptop computer. As his audit progressed, long strips of paper peeled smoothly and silently off the calculator and straggled over his work table. I looked up from time to time in envy and then down at my rattletrap manual typewriter, Royal by name but without an ounce of *noblesse oblige*. One day, after I had sighed loudly over a major erasure and had hurled a balled up, ruined carbon [expletives deleted] into the waste basket, Bonny looked up with a comment.

"Why don't you get a computer? A word processing program is so much easier than the antediluvian technology you're using. You're spending hours at a time, frustrated and aggravated, writing and revising, until you've achieved perfect wording and phrases. Doing that to an electronic copy is simple. So far, from what I see of your finances, you could certainly afford a computer. They're dirt cheap and so are the programs. Furthermore, the programs are easy to learn and use. Lots of bells and whistles, too. Say, wouldn't you like a built in thesaurus, and what about spell and grammar checks?"

"My spelling and grammar are very good, thank you. And I don't know that Horace Elder will be disposed to let go of thousands of dollars for what he probably considers my 'nice little hobby.' Besides, I'm not likely to be clever enough to profit from all those bells and whistles."

"Don't sell yourself short. You can type and you're smart in four languages, you can surely master word processing. If you want to consider it, let me get literature and prices for a set up that would meet your needs—a laptop computer, a printer, and a scanner wouldn't take anywhere near thousands of dollars. And a hookup to the Internet would be an inexpensive but very valuable resource for the work you do. Make a proposition to Elder in concrete terms. Can't get anywhere without trying. Whaddya say?"

I gave him a timid and highly tentative OK. I considered myself technologically challenged; I didn't even have a TV habit, the only sets in the house were Mrs. Bettle's and one in the servants hall. I was willing to think about contemporary conveniences but not necessarily to adopt them wholesale. Nevertheless, I sat down to my Royal pain again with some new ideas roaming around in my head. A thesaurus at my fingertips would be nice…

I thought even more seriously about computer-assisted writing when I got a letter from Marcus Atwater. It read:

Dear Ms. DeVille,

Please pardon my unpardonable delay in responding to your translations. I was out of the country when they arrived, then returned to suffer a bad bout of the flu. Only now am I working through the accumulation on my desk.

I was sorry to hear of Armand's circumstances. We were classmates at Harvard, you know, and co-founders of the short-lived Cosmos Club, which was dedicated to "bringing the ancient world to modern readers." I am delighted to know you are carrying on the tradition.

I was even more pleased to review what I consider your excellent renditions of three Greek comedies. Although I would occasionally quarrel with your reading of some words or phrases (a classicist's prerogative), I congratulate you on your ability to catch the flavor of the vulgar and bawdy aspects of the originals. Many of the thoroughly Bowdlerized translations fail miserably to communicate the vigor and liveliness of Greek drama. I regret I have no immediate opportunity to publish these offerings but I hope to receive more of them from you while I am seeking a sponsor for their publication. Please keep me in mind.

Very truly yours….

Maybe Atwater's letter would be ammunition to force a computer system out of Horace Elder, convince him that my work was more than a "nice little hobby," and might even promise modest remuneration. Bonny came back a week later with an itemized list, including prices, for an inexpensive but powerful combination of hardware and software. (I was beginning to get the lingo down although I had not yet conquered my qualms about venturing into unknown territory). When Ted returned from his business trip, he was enthusiastic as he scanned the brochures,

"Just the ticket for you. I'd want a set up like this if I weren't making my living on the road and making my home in a knapsack. Go for it!"

And in the end, I did—sent a letter with all the particulars to Elder, and wonder of wonders, he advanced the entire purchase price to the household account without cuts or demur. Bonny and Ted suspected a bribe to get me to back off from questioning his stewardship of the DeVille wealth. Ted was scheduled to leave for Guatemala the day after Christmas but the week before, he went to a computer store, bought the wherewithal, brought it home, installed it, and gave me rudimentary instructions for using it. Bonny signed me up for the Internet, had the phone company install a jack in the library, taught me how to e-mail his office with questions and information, and promised to back me up as I learned day-to-day word processing. As it happened, I was quick to master the basics of e-mail and the word processing program and by the first of February had managed to get about half of the current Ovid translation on disc. I was delighted with the flexibility I now had to rewrite, revise, and format my texts. The Royal was relegated to the top of the armoire and I began to entertain ambitions to copy to disc selected material that Papa and I had worked on together but I had never typed up. Bonny and Ted had both told me I could mail disc copies to Atwater, providing he had equipment and programs to read them. I wasn't that ambitious yet but I gloried in printing whatever I wanted in hard copy whenever I was ready. My musings at Papa's bedside now focused on enjoyable and productive hours away from it. I could keep dispassionate watch over Papa's face and body, eyes alert, mind elsewhere. I began to feel less aggrieved by my filial duties.

I noticed that Mrs. Bettle was recovering her character as a rosy-cheeked, starchly-uniformed version of the Pillsbury Doughboy, and Mrs. Ryan, although still tall, thin, and severe in her black silk dress, smiled more often. Pierce seemed not to change, at least in my presence, but fifty years of stiff-necked ceremonious behavior was not to be set aside lightly. Reducing the amount of time devoted to Papa's needs and achieving a distinctly less cranky attitude toward my life seemed to make a difference for everyone in the house. Roseanne's cheerful presence was recognized as a godsend, and her little sister had turned out to be a whiz-bang housemaid. When I stopped to think about my happier mindset, I attributed it as much to the new mood in the house as to improvement in my temper and temperament, although I didn't know which had come first.

§ Thirteen §

THE SNOWS CONTINUED. I kept up with my hair appointments, riding into the village in the grocery delivery van and back with Bonny. The roads were too treacherous for Pierce to get out the Cadillac. Dr. Eisenstein arrived for his monthly visits, driven by his son, Dr. Jake, in a four-wheel drive Blazer. While Dr. Eisenstein, Sr. checked Papa, Dr. Jake and I chatted over coffee and cinnamon rolls in the servants hall. The Eisensteins had attended our medical needs for as long as I could remember. Pierce had told me their story: Dr. E's parents emigrated from Austria as refugees in 1939, driven out by the rabid anti-Semitism of the era; they settled in the village, sponsored by the congregation of the First Methodist Church. Herr Doktor Professor Eisenstein, an outstanding physician and distinguished faculty member of the Medical School in Vienna, was not eligible to practice in the US. So he and his wife opened a coffee shop which became a social hub in the neighborhood. Mrs. (Rachel) baked the fantastically rich pastries characteristic of Vienna and Dr. (Itzhak) sold and served them at the counter. Their modest prosperity put son Lev in medical school, and started a dynasty of village medical care; daughter Leah practiced dentistry and the younger son, Hagen, opened the village pharmacy. The current generation had followed in the hard-working, socially conscious traditions of their forebears and people of all ages and incomes in the community venerated the name of Eisenstein. Dr. Lev had been elected county coroner repeatedly over the past thirty years. It was Lev, now on the verge of retirement, who had attended Papa for the last 15 years, after the high priced specialists had given up on him. When visiting, Dr. Lev mostly conferred with Mrs. Bettle, checked the care log, examined Papa for bedsores, renewed the prescriptions that kept him alive, and reported "No change, either for better or worse." Jake, with whom I was chatting, was a pediatrician and a bachelor. I think Mrs. Ryan had her eye on him as a potential match for me, but I was matchproof despite all her hints. Not that Jake was not a catch, he was a really nice fellow, but he was just not a catch I had in mind.

Jake was an enthusiastic computer owner and user and raved on at every opportunity about the benefits of technology to medicine and secondarily to civilization in general. When the Eisensteins were leaving after their March visit, Jake stopped by the library to admire my hardware and to congratulate me on my entrance to the 21st century, and incidentally, to invite me to dinner and a movie Saturday next. I was tempted, but second thoughts about the difficulty of rearranging watch shifts led to "No, thanks for asking." Jake nodded in friendly understanding, and I saw him off with regret. Although I had no aspirations to match up with him, a social evening in his company would have been agreeable. A familiar wave of bitter resentment at the filial duties that kept me from accepting his invitation washed over me. But the habit of civility and good manners prevailed once more as I turned away from the front door and swallowed my irritation without even a grimace.

§ Fourteen §

As I reentered the library Bonny was lying back in his chair rubbing his eyes. He looked up with a smile and a cheerful greeting. The table in front of him was piled high with Mrs. Ryan's quarterly reports of household expenses for the past 25 years and with file folders containing Elder's reports for the past five years. By now he had opened all of the sealed envelopes, although he had not yet worked on their contents in detail.

"Taking a break?" I asked.

"Just resting my eyes for a moment. You know, Clio, I may have happened on something. I'll have to do more probing before I'm sure but I have a question for you. On what day of the month does your allowance come?"

"What allowance? I've never had an allowance. I just ask Mrs. Ryan for what I need for my personal expenses and she gives me cash—out of the household money, I guess. I never asked. Why?"

"The trust instrument provides for a monthly allowance to be paid to you after your 21st birthday. The annual reports from Elder's office over the last 15 years show monthly payments of $600 to a bank account in your name. May I see your bank statements and check books?"

I stood dumbfounded.

"I don't have any bank records, never have had. I've always just asked Mrs. Ryan for money that I need for personal items and she gives it to me. I think she records it in her expense book but I've never written a check. Don't even have a checkbook. What in the world? I've never wanted for anything, although I must admit my wants have been minimal. A couple of $20 bills cover the little bit of shopping and my regular hair care. If I buy clothes or shoes, I use the household credit card; my dental and medical fees have always been billed directly to Elder's office. What do you mean?"

Perplexity and shock had raised the level of my voice to unwonted heights.

"Don't hurry to get bent out of shape over this. Maybe there's a perfectly reasonable explanation. Perhaps you could ask Mrs. Ryan what she knows about it. I will admit that $7200 *per annum* over 15 years adds up to quite a bit of money, over $100,000 in fact, and that certainly calls for explanation."

"I'm going to ask her right now," I flung myself toward the door but slowed down as Bonny said, "Take it easy, take ten deep breaths, and ask your questions calmly. You don't want her to think you are accusing her of mishandling funds. After all, she has been a long-time trusted servant with this family and a good friend to you as well."

His advice struck me as golden and I kept hold on my composure as I went to find Mrs. Ryan. She was polishing the dining room table, grumbling under her breath that the girls didn't put enough elbow grease into the job and if she didn't follow up on their work the house would be a pig sty. She looked up and put down her polish cloth as I came in, and as was her way, gave me her full attention. She always treated me as if I were mistress of the house even though I could take no credit for the running of it.

"Mrs. Ryan, I want to.... I need to...." I couldn't find the words, so I blurted out my question in hasty, ill-chosen words,

"Where do you get the money you give me for haircuts and clothes when I go to the village?"

She stiffened and flushed. Her voice and gaze grew sharp, "Why do you ask? I always give you whatever you ask for, do I not? Isn't it enough? Do you want more?"

"No, I'm sorry to be blunt, Mrs. Ryan, but the documents Mr. Harvill is reviewing refer to a bank account in my name. I have never known about it, and I need to know if it's the source of the funds you have been providing to me."

"I know nothing of a bank account in your name. The cash I've given you has always come out of the petty cash drawn from the household expense fund. That's why I always insist you give me the receipts for your purchases When you use the credit card, payment is charged against household expenses. I hope that Mr. Harvill isn't accusing me of fiddling the accounts. I've handled the household money for the last 25 years, recorded every cent in my ledgers, and there's never been a question. Why now?"

The flush on her face had faded to an ashen white and her voice trembled as she spoke. I was horrified that my clumsy inquiries had upset her. My emotions got the better of me and tears started to flow.

"I'm so sorry, Mrs. Ryan," I blubbered. "I could never suspect you of doing anything wrong. You and Pierce have always been my best friends. I've trusted my life and welfare to the two of you for all of my life and I'm not about to stop now. Please don't be upset. It's just that we have to know."

She rushed to my side and wrapped her arms around me.

"Oh, Miss Clio, dear girl, don't cry. I can only tell you the truth and show that Mr. Harvill my books. There hasn't been a cent spent out of this house that hasn't been recorded. Money spent on the house, without my management, has all come out of Mr. Elder's office."

In her distress, she forgot herself, picked up her polish cloth and wiped my tears away with it. The Lemon Pledge brought on a sneezing fit and she snatched it away in horror, then smiled, abashed, as I laughed away my tears and hugged her. She followed me back into the library and when Bonny leaped politely to his feet, offered him full access to her ledgers. She would have Pierce bring them out of the storage closet where they had been accumulating for 25 years and shelve them in the library. She explained that papers filed in the cabinet were quarterly summaries she had prepared and sent to Elder's office, where they had been reviewed, initialed, and returned. Bonny's face was a mixture of awe at the volume of original material at his command and gratitude for her generous co-operation.

§ FIFTEEN §

SPRING CAME LATE and with it Walter's resignation. He was going to farm by day and work a night shift at the cheese factory for better benefits and higher wages. He urgently needed to get a handle on his debts, Evvy was pregnant again. We contacted the Medical Employment Agency and they sent us Arnold Slocum, LPN. Mrs. Bettle explained that LPN stood for "licensed practical nurse;" after a week's trial, she pronounced him fully competent. He arrived with a wide-screen TV for which Mrs. Ryan had to order a cable jack installed in Ted's former room, and a flashy motorcycle of gargantuan proportions which we allowed him to stable in the garage. He spent his off-duty hours sleeping and watching TV in his room or tinkering in the garage. No one minded much since in company, he was rather surly, given to gloomy silences spiked with occasional outbursts of unfunny humor with a distinctly off-color tinge. He was tall and muscular, with the face of a former boxer, broken nose and all, but Mrs. Bettle was grateful for his strength. Handling Papa for bathing and change of bed linens was growing ever more difficult but now she could have Arnold's help at the morning and evening shift changes. Pierce, however, was as nervous as a long-tailed cat in a roomful of rocking chairs every time Arnold headed for the garage. Arnold was in love with machinery and hoped with his whole soul to get his hands on our 1964 Cadillac Brougham, which was the apple of Pierce's eye. He kept the car doors locked and the keys in his pocket in order to ensure no meddling behind his back

We had had several postcards from Ted. One pictured

Chichen'Itza, and promised lots of tales when he got home. Another showed a magnificent tropical beach; postmarked from a place we had never heard of; the message was "*Just out after a few days in jail. American consul very helpful.*" The latest was a picture of the Gatun Lock of the Panama Canal; "*WOW, what a place!!!!!!*" scrawled in the message space. He was obviously pursuing his goal with his usual verve and élan. We would be glad to greet his return.

And now to our misfortune, we learned that Bonny was *Captain* Harvill, US Marine Corps Reserve. That meant when he was called to active duty in Washington DC in June to work on a case of major malfeasance in a quartermaster's office, he left not knowing how long his stint would last. I missed him and his sunny presence at the table in the library, more than anyone else did. Further loss to our comfortable group occurred in July when Roseanne was whisked into marriage by her irate parents and dispatched with her soldier boy beau, now husband, to his station before she began to "show." Our regretful farewell, best wishes, a wedding gift of cash, and a baby-to-be gift of a car crib went with her.

Now the day shifts at Papa's bedside were again Mrs. Bettle's and my sole responsibility. The Medical Employment Agency told us they had currently no individuals in their listings who were both competent and willing to accept the terms and salary offered, but they would continue to seek a suitable care giver. Inquiries in the village had been fruitless. By the middle of August, three weeks of the old exhaustion and frustration that dogged Mrs. Bettle and me had taken their toll.

My work on the *Metamorphoses* had come to a standstill. When I tried to concentrate, I fell asleep over my keyboard and reference books. When I woke up from those uncomfortable minute-long naps, I was aware of aches and pains in my back and neck. I was tired and miserable all the time and the orbit of my morale was stuck in its nadir. When Pierce announced from the door,

"He's expecting you, Miss Clio,"

I answered "Thank you, Pierce. I'm going right up." and dragged myself up the stairs to meet Mrs. Bettle coming out of his room.

"I've given him his medication, Miss Clio. He ought to be asleep soon."

"Thank you, Mrs. Bettle," I replied.

Déjà vu all over again! Hate boiled up and burned in my throat like bile. But again, civility and good manners prevailed and I entered his room, my face carefully expressionless.

§ SIXTEEN §

THE NEXT MORNING I stood at a tower window finishing a cup of coffee. A violent thunderstorm in the night had followed a miserably muggy day, and the fresh, cool air was a delightful change. I saw the single taxi the village boasted coming up the long drive and pulling up in the circle at the front door. The passenger debarked—a short, fat man, rubicund face under a mane of white hair, nattily dressed and sporting an elegant cane, which he tapped on the pavement as the taxi driver pulled out a large leather suitcase, very handsome, and carried it to the doorstep. The fellow marched out of sight under the arch to the massive door and, disdaining the door bell button, vigorously thumped the heavy lion's head knocker. He chose to make his presence known with panache. I set down my cup and raced down the stair to the door to stop the loud noise that might set Papa off. I beat Pierce to the door by seconds, and opened it to hear,

"You must be Ms. Clio DeVille. Marcus Atwater here. Beautiful country around here and a most impressive house. "

Then apparently focusing on my stupefied countenance, he continued,

"Were you not expecting me? My letter was mailed a week ago to notify you that I was passing through Fairview on the way to a publisher's convention in Chicago, and that I planned to stop overnight with you, hoping to go over some of your work in progress. You seem surprised. Didn't you get my letter?"

It was a relief when he stopped to draw breath and I could get my ideas in order.

"No, we had no letter but you are welcome. Won't you come in?" and I led the way to the morning room while Pierce scurried to carry in the luggage and bring Mrs. Ryan up to speed on the latest development.

"Sorry to surprise you. However, in a big house like this with household staff, I daresay you can handle an unexpected guest. I'm not fussy, won't need fancy food or digs, just wanted to give your manuscripts a look, that is, if you'll permit. And a visit to Armand, so sad about him, the taxi driver told me about his condition and that there is no hope of recovery. I say, I'd like to freshen up. Could someone point me to a powder room?"

The man was a veritable talking machine. I led him out to the hall and gestured helplessly at the cloakroom door. While he was in there, I skipped out to catch Mrs. Ryan, who was already upstairs hustling the maids. There were plenty of bedrooms available but they were hardly fit for instant occupancy. There had not been an overnight guest in Hauteville House for ten or twelve years. I knew there would be plenty of clean bedding, and the bedroom Mrs. Ryan chose for Atwater would need no more than cursory dusting and vacuuming, but the girls were getting their orders.

"Get the windows open in the red bedroom, and pull the drapes back." Her voice was low but urgent, "Fresh linen on the bed and in the bathroom, water in a bedside carafe, exchange the spread for one from the linen closet, let the room air until evening. I'll need both of you to help me in the kitchen for lunch. Plan on staying to help for dinner too."

Mrs. Ryan may have been taken by surprise but she was determined to maintain the standards of the House, such as they were. I wondered if she was not actually enjoying laying on a lavish welcome for a house guest. When I returned to the morning room, Atwater was parading around eying the art hanging on the walls. He stood, head cocked to one side, enraptured by the

Cassatt, dismissing the Hassam with a neutral nod, and looking puzzled at a bright-colored daub in a narrow wood frame.

"I did that, age ten," I said. "My art tutor thought it was rather remarkable and so Mrs. Ryan, our housekeeper, framed it and, with my father's grudging permission, hung it here. It's really refrigerator door genre. It's a circus elephant."

"Why is it blue?"

"I had been taken to the circus where the elephants performed under blue lights and that must have made an impression on me. But tell me, how is it you were passing through Fairview? No rail or air connection within miles."

"Bus! Took the train to Erie and bussed from there. Going back the same way, will catch the train to get to Chicago day after tomorrow. I'm hoping to make some contacts at the convention with colleagues and acquaintances to push some of your translations. That was one reason for my dropping in here, I liked the samples you sent me, wanted to see more, wanted to look over some of Armand's work as well. He used to have a nice hand although he tended to be a bit pedantic. Breadth of knowledge was his forte, he could put every author in the right age, right country, and right city and create the color and ambience for the piece, if not in the translation *per se*, then in the footnotes, with which—to my mind—he was always a bit too generous."

My head was awhirl before he ran out of wind. What a talker! I took advantage of his temporary silence to suggest we adjourn to the library. I told him that lunch would be served at 11 A.M. after which I would be on watch duty until four P.M. I hoped he could entertain himself with the manuscripts and texts until dinner at seven. Then after dinner, if all went well with Papa, I would let him visit the sickroom before I went back on duty at eight. His face screwed up in an expression of sympathy as he came to an understanding of my commitment, but he did not comment.

"Fine, fine, libraries are my native heath, and I will be completely happy to pore over the contents of yours. Aha," he cried as we entered, "Wonderful, wonderful! I see many an old friend among your reference volumes. And you have a computer. I'm sure you are finding it very useful but I distrust them. Don't even hold with typewriters. I believe that writing by machine risks drying up the creative juices that flow more quickly and generously with pen in hand. I am myself unregenerate, write everything with my special fountain pen on yellow legal pads for my secretary to transform into print. Now then, where may I settle down and will someone call me to lunch when it's ready?"

I assured him Pierce would call him and lead him to the dining room. I showed him the stacks of manuscripts on the shelves of the armoire and moved my current work to Bonny's table so he could spread out at the desk. He would have had more to talk about but I escaped with the excuse to check on lunch preparations. The man wore me out!

§Seventeen §

WE LUNCHED IN the morning room on cream of broccoli soup, tomato cups stuffed with chicken salad, corn muffins, and fresh fruit compote. I hoped Atwater could not read into the menu the degree of unreadiness experienced in the kitchen. As we ate, I tried to keep the conversation steered in the direction of the *décor* of the morning room: chintz and white Italian wicker surviving from the Armand I era; a collection of fine paintings established in the Armand II phase (his choices, she looking the other way); the original architect's decision to create a wall of sunlight with French windows and doors. However, whenever I flagged, Atwater took over with encomiums over the treasures of the library. He was especially captivated by the variety and richness of the reference volumes; with a half-serious glint in his eye, he warned me to search him as he left—he coveted an 18th century printing of Erasmus's dictionary and an Aldine edition of Tasso. The manuscripts he had reviewed were wonderful, wonderful! Those bearing both Papa's and my touches were especially good—Armand's ripe knowledge and my youthful insights, wonderful, wonderful! Thank you, one cup of coffee only, can't take the time for a second, want to get back to the library.

And again, as he rolled off to rummage the armoire and shelved tomes, I was left exhausted by the spate of his words. I went up to Papa's room, however, with a new respect for Papa's talents. I was not the only person who respected his scholarly prowess. I was thinking of a quotation, maybe a scrap of Shakespeare, something about "how now is a noble mind o'erthrown." As I sat down in the watcher's chair, I gazed at the motionless form under the covers with pity, for all the wasted years, both his and mine.

At the end of my shift, I showered and dressed for dinner, then sent Pierce to warn Atwater that he would have to check his own timepiece for dinner at seven. The huge gong in the hall had been silenced in deference to Papa's sensitivity to loud noises. Mrs. Ryan had done wonders, a splendid dinner: an antipasto platter, pasta carbonara, beef roast garlanded with potatoes and carrots, Caesar salad, a Linzer torte for dessert (I suspected someone's fast trip to Eisenstein's to achieve that triumph). Normally parsimonious with the contents of the wine cellar, Pierce had brought out a red Rothschild to complement the beef and a delicate Rheinwein to go with the torte. Atwater must have impressed him with some tales of European travels. We dined *a deux* in the bay of the dining room, on the finest of our embroidered linens, china, crystal, and silver. My conviction grew that household staff was enjoying Atwater's visit a whole lot more than it had Elder's. Dinner entertainment consisted of an agreeable monologue describing Atwater's visits to European museums and biblioteca and his dining experiences in five-star French restaurants. He was amusing and I was tired enough to be grateful for the relief of effort to hold up my end of a conversation. He finally pushed back his chair from the table with a satisfied sigh, and patting his nicely rounded belly, said,

"Well, now, that was a wonderful dinner. Pierce, please convey my compliments to the cook. I would do so myself but I was hoping to make a visit to Armand's room with Miss Clio before she takes up her bedside watch. Shall we?"

I acquiesced and led the way upstairs. Mrs. Bettle had taken pains to have Papa and the room in good order and after cautioning Atwater to speak softly, I said to Papa,

"Papa, Mr. Marcus Atwater has come to say hello."

Papa's eyelids flickered but just barely. Atwater stepped close and looking down at Papa's stony face, whispered gently,

"Hello there, my friend. I came to visit, hoping for one of those good old arguments over the Greek aorist but I see you would rather not. Now that I have met your beautiful daughter, I must compliment you on her talents. She is worthy indeed to follow in your footsteps. I won't tire you with more chit chat. Good-bye for now."

And as he turned away, tears sliding down his cheeks, Papa's eyelids flickered again and his upper lip twitched. It was the most reaction he had shown in months. Mrs. Bettle ushered Atwater out and since it was eight P.M., I stayed to take up my station, promising to meet with Atwater the next morning after breakfast. His tears spoke more loudly than his flow of words ever would. I was glad he had come.

He and I spent the next morning over my Ovid-in-progress. He was complimentary of the work already done and made useful suggestions for the next phase. He wanted me to do the whole *Metamorphoses*; he thought it would sell better than a collection of selections. He had another idea which attracted me—interspersing the stories with explanatory commentary and fleshing them out with descriptions of the period and circumstances in which they were conceived and committed to writing. I would have to study an extensive body of references to do that but the challenge appealed to me.

Atwater had ordered up his taxi for 11 A.M., in time to catch the noon bus to Erie. He refused a sit down lunch but accepted Mrs. Ryan's offer of a box lunch composed of cold roast beef sandwiches, an orange, and a generous piece of Linzer torte. He went off in fine fettle, still talking up a storm, as jaunty as a robin on the lawn, promising to stay in touch. He had worn me out and I had to fight to stay awake on my afternoon watch shift. So I was shaken to my soul to hear a sepulchral voice,

"You're a good daughter, Clio."

I leaped to my feet and bent close over the motionless face on the bed, but there was nothing more, only the usual even breathing and closed lids, I wasn't ready to believe my ears until I had told Mrs. Bettle when she came in for her shift.

"I thought his eyes were brighter last evening but of course, he didn't speak. That Mr. Atwater's visit must have wakened something in his mind. I'm glad it was you he spoke to."

And then she went placidly on with her preparations for his evening feeding.

§ Eighteen §

Time passed with no visible change in Papa's state. In three months, we had endured four live-in nurse's aides; Mrs. Bettle and I agreed that was almost as stressful as our old schedule. Two of them seemed to begrudge the kind of care necessary for Papa's comfort and cleanliness, and everything they did was slipshod and had to be done over. Dismissing them was both a relief and an aggravation, good riddance and a need to start all over on a frustrating search for replacements. The third had flung out in high dudgeon in the middle of a shift, claiming the accommodations were beneath her standards and the food wasn't fit to eat. We suspected the fourth drank and of course, firing her was unavoidable. Arnold soldiered on keeping his night watch faithfully and roaring off on his motorcycle in the daytimes when he wasn't watching television. We had a letter from Bonny saying his job in DC would wind up a week before Thanksgiving, we should expect him back at his old stand the day after.

The Medical Employment people finally sent us another nurse's aide, a grandmotherly type named Mrs. Wiggs, who was completely satisfactory as a care-giver and a genuinely nice person. But she was so talkative at mealtimes that the rest of us, whenever our meals coincided with hers, gobbled our food at express train speed and then ran. Mrs. Wiggs brought her television set and Mrs. Ryan had had to get a cable jack in another room in the east wing. Expanding staff was money in the bank for the cable company. Mrs. Wiggs and Mrs. Bettle found common ground in their devotion to soap operas. Although their staggered hours rarely permitted them to see the same episodes, they shared news of their favorite characters whenever they could. By the last week of November, a degree of peace and tranquil routine had returned to Hauteville House. Bonny was back at his table, punching the keys of his calculator and laptop and I was back at my desk working on backgrounds for the Ovid stories. Warned by Marcus Atwater, I avoided footnotes and concentrated on the essays that would introduce or trail a translated segment.

Ted arrived two days before Christmas and went to stay with the Bigelows until Arnold departed on a two-week vacation, at which time Ted took over not only the night watch but not Arnold's room. Ted's tales of his adventures preempted Mrs. Wiggs's ramblings; his yarns were so interesting she just listened open-mouthed. "I never knew a world traveler before," she breathed. Christmas week and New Year's were festive; the house smelled of evergreens, roasting fowl, and mince pies. Mistletoe hanging from the hall chandelier was Ted's favorite decoration; he captured every female in the house at every opportunity and took the toll of a kiss. Lily and Clara were in a permanent giggle and even Mrs. Ryan blushed and smiled when she was caught.

It was again a time of respite, the weather, though cold, spared us heavy snows until mid-January. Bonny was back on his old schedule and Ted had again taken up his temporary quarters at the Bigelows. Then Arnold came down with the flu. That was the beginning of momentous events, and a return to overtime watches for Mrs. Bettle, Mrs. Wiggs, and me. The last Saturday in January, Mrs. Bettle had just completed an uneventful night shift by feeding and bathing Papa and changing the linens. I took up my station and thanked my lucky stars that I had asked Mrs. Ryan to call the Bigelows to see if Ted could help out until Arnold was healthy again. I checked the contents of the vial of medication on the bedside table; it was full. Our routine was to set out a new vial when we had taken the final dose from the last. We would remove the seal and take off the metal cap that protected the rubber diaphragm stoppering the vial; lay out a fresh syringe with its sheathed needle attached; and place a pledget of cotton on the alcohol dispenser—everything ready for immediate action. Mrs. Bettle had left everything in order and I sat back on my chair and let my mind roam over my plans for the next bout of translating.

Hearing the telltale sounds of the beginning of a seizure, I drew up the standard dose from the vial and injected it as per routine. I stood by, expecting relief of the seizure within the usual three to four minutes, and when it did not occur, administered a second dose, according to Dr. Eisenstein's instructions. Only rarely was a second dose necessary, but when it was, it was effective—but not this time. Again following Dr. Eisenstein's instructions, I hurried to the stock of medication kept in a small refrigerator in the bathroom, took out an unopened vial, unsealed it, drew up a dose and administered it. By this time, Papa's lips and fingertips were going blue and his breath was rattling in his throat. I ran to pound on Mrs. Bettle's door. She came out, wearing her robe and slippers, and raced with me to Papa's bedside. The third dose of medication was beginning to have an effect and the blue was fading from his lips. As she checked Papa's vital signs, she ordered me to get on the phone and call Dr. Lev.

"Tell him, Mr. DeVille's respirations are rapid and his heart rate is fast and erratic, both systolic and diastolic blood pressure are low. He'll come with the right equipment and meds. Hurry!"

My call was put through to Dr. Benazir, the Pakistani physician Dr. Lev had recently taken into the practice. Dr. Ben, as people had begun to call him, asked a number of questions, then told me to keep Papa warm, watch him closely for respiratory arrest, and do CPR if it occurred. He and Dr. Lev would be with us as soon as they had assembled appropriate gear and meds and could make the trip. I relayed his advice to Mrs. Bettle, who was still taking vital signs every few minutes, and then retreated to the hall to sit on a big old chest, ready to run downstairs to the phone if necessary. Pierce came hurrying up the back stairs, asking what the trouble was and what he could do. I filled him in and sent him to suggest that Mrs. Ryan get some hot water bottles ready. He returned in ten minutes, bearing four tightly-capped bottles labeled Apollo Spring Water and carefully arranged on a napkin on a tray. The sight of him and his burden almost drove me to hysterical laughter but instead, I just said,

"Wha-a-at????"

"We didn't have any hot water bottles, Miss Clio, so we filled these from the hot water tap until we could do better."

"Yes, thank you, Pierce. I'll take them. Why don't you go to the front door, the doctors will be coming very soon."

I took the tray into Papa's room and gave it into Mrs. Bettle's keeping. She said the bottles would do just fine and wrapping them in towels, placed them around Papa's body. Papa's breathing had steadied and she asked me to stay close while she took a minute to put on her uniform and shoes before the doctors came.

I watched them arrive from the landing. They stamped the snow from their feet and handed their coats to Pierce. Together with their bags, they carried cases of what I assumed were monitoring and testing equipment. I beckoned them up the stairs and they entered Papa's room, telling me to wait outside. Before I resumed my seat on the old chest, I went to my room for a heavy sweater. Now that the excitement had faded, I was cold to the core, even though the house was its normal cozy temperature.

Dr. Ben emerged first, his dark face serious and his heavy brows drawn together in a frown.

"I'm afraid, Miss Clio, the attack has been very critical, such that the heart has been severely stressed. We have given Mr. DeVille medication to strengthen his heartbeat and restore it to normal rhythm but he will take careful nursing. Mrs. Bettle will need to remain in constant attendance in order to administer the new medications. We recommend you make arrangements to bring in another registered nurse to relieve her from time to time. I understand the night nurse is ill and the nurse's aide is not certified to administer medication other than in emergency."

I nodded and looked up as Dr. Lev came out. His face too was serious.

"Clio, our prognosis is not good but for the moment, his condition is stable. Now, I want you to tell me exactly how all the problems started."

I noticed that he held in his hand a Kleenex in which he had enclosed the two vials from which I had given the doses. I related the exact sequence of the first dose at the beginning of the seizure from an unsealed but full vial, the second dose from the same vial, then the third dose from a full vial taken from the stock supply, seal intact until I ripped it open.

"Now, then, I intend to take these vials and the entire current stock of this medication with me. It would appear that the contents of the ineffective vial were either bad from the maker or have gone bad on the shelf. Whatever the case, we need to investigate and replace it with fresh product of a different lot number. I'll be calling the pharmacy and Hagen will rush the new stuff to you. In the meantime, I've instructed Mrs. Bettle and now you or any other care-giver to use only from the new supply. I'll need a small box or bag to carry away the stuff on hand."

I sent Pierce for a suitable box and he went off to the east wing, returning with a fancy flowered paper gift bag, and saying he couldn't find a box, would this do. I was beginning to think that for house staff creative substitutions were becoming routine, but what the hey, whatever worked was OK. As soon as the doctors left, I was on the phone to get qualified nurses on the scene. I had to settle for off-duty nurses from the hospital in a patchwork of coverage. As I drooped wearily over the phone, arrangements made, I recollected I ought to let Mr. Elder in on the situation. Elder was out of the office, his secretary took the message.

§ Nineteen §

THE REST OF the morning passed with Mrs. Bettle whispering periodic reports at his bedroom door, Papa's vital signs were holding. I called Ted to tell him what had happened and that his services were not needed. I also called Bonny with my tale of events, in case he preferred not to come. He was understanding but didn't see any reason to stay away; he wouldn't need me as he worked and he urged me to rest as much as I could. One of the relief nurses came at noon and took up watch after Mrs. Bettle had passed on the doctors' orders. When Bonny arrived in the early afternoon, he brought his spare cell phone, thinking it would be useful in an emergency in the sickroom. I blessed him for his thoughtfulness and the nurses did too; they had dreaded a run down the stairs to the phone in the hall for emergency contact to a doctor. Mrs. Ryan was still carrying chicken soup and crackers to Arnold at intervals and describing his misery. I regretted forgetting to ask the doctors to see him while they were here, but I expected one or both of them back in the evening and would bring Arnold's plight to their attention then. About three o'clock I shed my clothes for a nightgown and crawled into bed for a nap. Waked by knocking on my door, I looked blearily at the bedside clock—nine P.M., and Pierce's voice telling me Dr. Ben was here seeing Papa. Hastily, I donned robe and slippers, ran a comb through my hair, and hurried out into the hall.

"He's holding his own," Dr. Ben soothed. "I'm encouraged. How are you doing?"

"Thank you for the good news, and for coming. I'm doing OK.

You must have had a busy day. While you are here, would you mind attending our night nurse who is down with the flu? I forgot all about him this morning, except for ordering everyone in contact with him to stay away from Papa."

Dr. Ben cheerfully agreed and followed Pierce to Arnold's room in the east wing. When he returned, he said he had left antihistamine tablets and cough lozenges, the only treatment for a viral flu. He heartily endorsed frequent applications of chicken broth and suggested adding milk puddings as tolerated, but cautioned me not to expect Arnold to return to duty for at least two weeks. For a moment I thought he was going to make an additional observation but instead, he only said he or Dr. Lev would look in on Arnold when they returned to see Papa, probably tomorrow afternoon. After Pierce had shown Dr. Ben out, he came to tell me that Mr. Elder had called at 5:15, but when told I was resting, said he would call back in the morning. Elder told Pierce he had called Dr. Lev to get official word on Papa's condition. I was grateful to have time to gather my thoughts before I had to deal with Horace Elder. When I went back to my room, I peered long and hard into my mirror. Even by the soft light of the side lamps, I looked terrible—the black rings were back under my eyes, my skin was bleached colorless, and my forehead and temples were seamed with worry wrinkles. My nap had done little for my looks and less for my peace of mind. After one last visit to Papa's door and a quick report from the nurse, I returned to bed and slept in a turmoil of ugly dreams. I woke at dawn, stupid and dull, but after showering and washing my hair, dressing in my nicest jeans and shirt, getting the latest report on Papa, I went down for breakfast and ate with a surprisingly good appetite. It was as if I were starting over, yesterday and its commotions behind me, nowhere to look except ahead.

I was ready and primed for Elder's call when it came at ten o'clock. After polite greetings, he said, "Doctor Eisenstein advised me to stand ready in case Armand's condition worsened but said I need not come to Hauteville House at this time. I will stay in close contact with the doctors and with you, of course, in the meantime. I have authorized funds for the extraordinary expenses of his care temporarily but I strongly advise you to transfer him to a hospital or to a nursing home. Institutional care would not only be in his best medical interests, but would also be most economical of resources in the long run. I will continue to check with Dr. Eisenstein to learn when Armand can be moved and will then make the arrangements."

I could feel my face burning red with my anger, *economical* indeed! He didn't give a tinker's damn about Papa's wellbeing. Just the bottom line on a bank statement. With a major effort of will, I bit my tongue to reply calmly,

"Both doctors believe moving him would kill him. I believe it is my decision, in consultation with the physicians, to make. And I *will* have him stay here, where he's lived all his life, well or ill, with the care I can give and supervise. Please do not bring up the subject again."

I could hear Elder's deep-drawn breath as he started on lame excuses, humming and hawing, voicing his insincere concern to save me the worry and stress of constant care. There was little more conversation but I hung up feeling I had won this skirmish. I told Bonny of Elder's emphasis on the economics of keeping Papa at home, and boasted my minor victory. Bonny's reaction surprised me.

"He may well have reason to worry about money. I went to a meeting of corporate accountants last week. When an old buddy of mine heard I was doing an audit on Elder's management of a client account, he tipped me a wink and swore me to secrecy on a bit of gossip he had picked up. Namely, Mrs. Elder Number Three has filed for divorce and plans to take old Horace to the cleaners. She's got a court order to audit his personal and business holdings, and although he's fighting it and may have a decent chance to win, he's between a rock and a hard place. Add to that what I *think* I'm turning up in my audit of DeVille affairs, Horace Elder may be pretty nervous."

"What *are* you turning up?" I asked. "We haven't talked about things for quite a while. I wasn't sure you had anything to tell me."

"Well, I haven't found a smoking gun, but I have reached a point where I am obliged to advise you to hire a smart, honest lawyer who knows how to use a smart, honest, private investigator to follow up on your ghostly bank account. I'm convinced the smoking gun exists, but I'm not the one with the means to bring it into the open."

I groaned, "Who is? I don't know any lawyer, much less a smart, honest one. And if I did, how would I pay him or her?"

"Try a handshake agreement, on spec, like we have. I can assure you that any settlement in your favor will put you in control of plenty of money for topnotch legal advice. I've studied the holdings in the trust, and in the years since it was set up, it has been well-managed by the bank; the capital investments have prospered from canny buying and selling and an occasional stock split. It's the payouts into Elder's hands that have fallen into murky waters. And those payouts are what Elder collects and manages; I'm also seeing some dubious investments that seem to have been ill chosen and badly handled."

I groaned again, put my head in my hands, and gave myself up to despair.

"Look, do you trust me enough to let me recommend a lawyer? If your father is not likely to survive very much longer, you need to think about someone to defend your interests. I know of a firm in Erie that I would take my own legal troubles to, if I had any. It is an old firm, founded by a friend of my grandfather, has a stainless reputation for integrity and putting clients' interests first, no matter what. If you want me to get in touch with it on your behalf, I'll ask them to contact you. What say?"

I said please do, more in desperation than in hope. Then I donned boots, parka, muffler, bonnet, and mittens and went for a walk in the bright sunshine and cold, cold air. I saw a cardinal flaunting his scarlet crest in a leafless oak, teased by a squirrel chattering insults; below, the snow was marked by rabbit tracks and an owl feather; and a wild holly bush covered with bright red berries etched a bright picture under the blue sky. For a little while I liked the world I lived in.

§ Twenty §

Over the next few days, Papa's cardiac function grew slowly, steadily, irreversibly worse. I was spending an hour or so morning, afternoon, and evening with him and the nurse on duty. There was nothing for me to do, but whether it was habit or a sense of duty, I felt compelled to spend some time near him. I was called away one afternoon by Pierce informing me that Ms. Susan LeMoine had arrived for our conference and was waiting in the morning room.

As I entered the room I saw Ms. LeMoine from the back against the light from the French windows, a figure in scarlet wool, slender as a reed, no taller nor older than I, hemline mid-thigh, black patent leather boots to the knee. She turned and presented a long oval face the color of *café au lait*, a cap of tight black curls, and black eyes of such penetrating intelligence they almost frightened me. She strode toward me, hand outstretched.

"How do you do, Ms. DeVille, I'm Susan LeMoine, from Magnin, Jones, and Belowitz."

Her voice, a rich contralto, was as striking as her gaze. I shook the outstretched hand and indicated chairs at the table where she had already deposited her patent leather briefcase. I asked if she would like some refreshment.

"Thank you, no. Your butler has already asked. I'm here to find out what you want from legal counsel and if you want it from our firm. I can fill you in with some information about it. Magnin is dead, Jones and Belowitz are second generation from the founding partners. We have 15 attorneys on staff, with varied backgrounds and areas of expertise. I was assigned to confer with you because of a possibility of litigation over financial matters, that being my forte."

She sat back in her chair, ready to listen. Problem was, I didn't know what to say. So I asked, "What do you know of my concerns so far?"

She seemed to understand my confusion and to my great relief, took control of the conversation.

"Not much. But I can wing it until I have found out why you think you might need legal counsel. What I do know is that you are the only heir of your father, that he has been ill for years, and had placed a general power of attorney over the family affairs in the hands of a lawyer named Horace Elder. Mr. Harvill told me you are facing your father's imminent demise, with apprehensions about the family's financial status. How might our firm help you?"

"May I ask first what is a 'general' power of attorney? That term is unfamiliar to me and maybe I should understand it before we go on."

"A general power of attorney is authorization to act for someone in every aspect of his affairs, from handling investments to management of funds. I had an impression that Mr. Elder has been operating under a general power of attorney for 10 to 15 years."

"Thank you for that explanation. The use or misuse of that power is what concerns me. I want to know if Papa's lawyer has used his power of attorney dishonestly or unwisely or both. I want to know how I can deal with my distrust of Horace Elder and cope with difficulties that are sure to arise upon Papa's death. I want to know how to go on with *my* life when it is no longer controlled by Papa's attorney and the circumstances of Papa's illness. I must, however, be forthright with you. I have no money of my own at this time. I probably have 'expectations' but no idea of how great they might be. Any commitment I make to your firm would have to be a handshake and $1 retainer such as I have with Bonny Harvill...."

Just then Pierce erupted into the room, his voice a quaver,

"Miss Clio, come! Come! Mrs. Bettle says you have to come right now. She's already called the doctors. He...he's very bad."

"I'm coming. Please show Ms. LeMoine to the library, and ask Mr. Harvill to give her any information she wants. Excuse me...."

And I rushed up the stairs to find Mrs. Bettle standing beside the bed, holding Papa's hand, slow tears running down her plump cheeks, "I've done what I can but I think this is the end. What shall I do now?"

Taking Papa's other hand, I said, "We'll wait and speak softly and gently over him. Perhaps he will know from our voices that we are here to bid him farewell and help him through the door to the next world."

"What shall I say?" she sobbed.

"Try your favorite hymn. I know what I'm going to say." And I started with the first text Papa taught me to translate. I could still hear his sonorous rendering of *Arma virumque cano, Troiae qui primus ab oris Italiam, fato profugus Laviniaque venit litora—multum ille et terris iactatus et alto vi superum......*

As the stately Latin iambs rolled off my tongue, tears rolled down my face, and a burden of hate seemed to roll off my heart. Aeneas had fulfilled his fate on the shores of Latium and Papa had reached his fated destination after as many tribulations.*

* Opening words of the Aeneid, Book I: Arms I sing and the man who first from the coasts of Troy, exiled by fate, came to Italy and Lavinian shores; much buffeted on sea and land by violence from above....*

§ Twenty Two §

When Dr. Lev had completed the final official examinations of Papa's body, he came to me and put his arm around me.

"You have my sympathy, Clio. His death was an easy one after a very hard life. Grieve for what was good and now is gone, forget everything else."

"Thank you," I said, replying dry-eyed, "but what do I do now? I've never dealt with death. I don't know what I ought to do, he never talked about dying, never said what he wanted...."

"I'm sure he left a will, I was witness to it years ago. He probably left the will and instructions for his final rites with Mr. Elder. I'll call Elder if you want me to and he can arrange everything for you. I'll get the death certificate to the mortician when the choice has been made and bring you a copy for your records as well. Don't worry about anything now. OK?"

I nodded and escorted him to the front door where Pierce stood holding his hat and coat, a look of terrible loss on his face. I remembered that Pierce had been a boot boy on the household staff when Papa was born and now here he was at his death—the span of a life within the years of his own. After I said goodbye to Dr. Lev, I put my arms around Pierce and kissed his wrinkled cheek. A single sob escaped him and then he resumed his customary expressionless dignity.

"Ms. LeMoine is still here," he said in a shaky voice. "With Mr. Harvill in the library."

"Thank you, Pierce. I'll go in."

Bonny and Ms. LeMoine sat at Bonny's table, a selection of documents laid out in front of them. They rose as I entered.

"I'm sorry," I said, "but...."

"We know, Pierce told us. It is we who are sorry." Bonny said. Both he and Ms. LeMoine expressed their sympathy. I thanked them for their condolences, and after an uncomfortable moment of silence, I said to Ms. LeMoine,

"I will definitely need your services. Can I engage them with a handshake and a retainer? Now that Papa is dead, does Elder still have power of attorney?"

"No, the power of attorney died with your father. However, it's highly probable that Elder has been named executor of the will and consequently is enabled to act in the immediate aftermath of his death. I presume he will make the funeral arrangements on your behalf. I will look into the situation discreetly and take whatever steps you authorize."

I thanked her and went out to raid the paper boy's money in the drawer of the hall table for a dollar bill. Handshake and receipt executed, she wrote her home and cell phone numbers on the back of her business card, encouraged me to call her any time, and bade us goodbye. Bonny left with a friendly hug soon after. And I stood there, empty handed, my mind a blank, wondering what to do next. My problem was solved when Mrs. Ryan came to me. Her usually stern face was blotched with the tears she had shed and wiped away, but she had her emotions under control when she put her arms around me in a loving embrace.

"Miss Clio, I'm so sorry, but we have to go on, don't we? I'm ready to do anything you want me to, just tell me. It's all yours now."

Yes, I thought, everything's mine now, and everything's going to be different. Without Papa—no longer will the daily schedule revolve around his bedside; no longer will my life be tied to keeping watch and keeping watchers on duty. Today brings all new responsibilities—welcome distractions from sad old preoccupations. I blessed Mrs.. Ryan silently for recalling me to my new duties. With a sharp intake of breath, I took the plunge.

"First, Mrs. Ryan, I expect Mr. Elder will be arriving soon to make funeral arrangements. Have the red bedroom made up for him. He may bring an assistant or secretary with him so you might prepare for an additional guest as well. We probably need to get several days provisions in for guests and staff and have the maids work full-time for the time being. You'll need their help in the kitchen. Mrs. Bettle, Mrs. Wiggs, and Arnold will be welcome to stay on in the house until they decide to leave after the funeral. I'll ask Mrs. Bettle to call the hospital nurses and cancel their engagements; Elder will mail them their checks. And I'll have Mrs. Bettle clear out the medical supplies from Papa's room; then you can have the girls give it a thorough cleaning. Oh, I expect there should be a reception of some kind here at the House after the funeral service; we may have to freshen the china, crystal, and table linens, and polish silver. When the arrangements have been settled, I will sit down to write invitations to Ted, Bonny, the Bigelows, the Starks, the Eisensteins, Mr. Atwater—and if you think of anyone else in the meantime, please remind me."

I ran out of breath and ideas at the same time. Mrs. Ryan had absorbed all of my instructions and I could count on her memory and her execution of them to be perfect. She had one question,

"How long do you think Arnold will be staying? He's much better but not well enough to go riding off on that motorcycle without a home to go to."

"He'll stay as long as Dr. Lev thinks he should. He does have a home to go to, his sister lives in Erie and that was the home address he gave on his application."

"And Mrs. Bettle and Mrs. Wiggs?"

"I'll leave it up to Mrs. Bettle to say when she wants to leave; I won't hurry her, this has been her home for so many years. I expect Mrs. Wiggs will go after the funeral. I'll try to get Mr. Elder to authorize appropriate severance pay for them and Arnold; they deserve something extra for their faithful service."

Mrs. Ryan nodded in agreement and bustled off to start her preparations. We had had our conversation in the library and now I dropped into my desk chair and leaned back, tired to the bone—and hungry! I suddenly realized I had not had lunch. The thought of a sandwich and a cup of coffee restored my energy and I rose and headed for the kitchen. Back to the basics of living was another distraction to be welcomed.

§ Twenty Two §

That afternoon I stood in the hall with the household staff in a reverent line as the mortician's men carried down the gurney bearing the neatly shrouded mound of Papa's long body. Even Arnold had risen shakily from his sickbed to be present. Mrs. Wiggs choked back noisy sobs and Mrs. Bettle blew her nose often but quietly. The rest of us were silent; the silence of Mrs. Ryan and Pierce was more poignant than their tears would have been. Pierce closed the door with an air of finality after the procession had passed through and we all scattered to our various tasks. I took a call from Mr. Elder's secretary informing me he would be arriving tomorrow for a stay of several days; he would be accompanied by a junior member of his office staff, a Mr. Thomas Gordon. Would accommodations at Hauteville House be available for both or should she arrange something in the village. I assured her expectant pause that we could handle both guests and would be ready for them whenever they arrived and however long they proposed to stay.

When they came, it was in a brand new Cadillac Eldorado, deep dark blue, spotlessly clean, gleaming with chrome. Mr. Gordon was apparently gofer, chauffeur, and secretary since he had driven the car, and now carried in all of the luggage and briefcases. He was very tall, lanky, not young, his shock of blond hair streaked with grey, his craggy face wearing a tentative but pleasant smile. Elder addressed perfunctory condolences and an introduction to me, then went on to say,

"Tom here has been point man on Armand's affairs for the last few months and his help in clearing up the estate will be invaluable. I'll leave it to you to get him settled and I'll get on the arrangements with the undertaker. I chose Mallory over in Deerfield because he's close. Armand's instructions specify cremation and a memorial service with a limited number of guests. I think the service ought to be held here, the cremains displayed in the drawing room, overflow seating in the hall. Can your staff handle that? Mallory's men can manage extra chairs and rearranging furniture...."

" Yes, yes, the House staff can cope with whatever arrangements we work out with Mr. Mallory. Reverend McLinn will say a few words at the memorial service; I have specified the service to be kept short. There will be a reception in the dining room afterwards. After you and Mr. Mallory have settled on time for the service, a container for the ashes, and appropriate payment, ask him to consult me or Mrs. Ryan on further details. As to scheduling the service, suggest a week from today, since I need to have time enough to get out formal invitations to the guests. Thank you for making the initial contact with Mr. Mallory but I would prefer that he would deal directly with us from now on. I expect you will handle selection of a simple container for the ashes and payment for his services."

I had made up my mind to control as much of the affair taking place on Hauteville House premises as I could. So I intended to get my decisions on record at the outset. I strove for a voice firm enough to forestall any argument. I must have succeeded, the tone of Elder's answer was placatory.

"Uh, er, yes, of course. Armand wanted his ashes to be interred in the family cemetery but Mallory insists on waiting until the spring thaw and easier access with his machinery. In the meantime, Mallory can give the urn into your keeping or can store it at the mortuary. Which would you prefer?"

"I'll have him store it. When spring comes, I'll contact him for the interment. Now is there anything else we have to deal with right away? If not, Mrs. Ryan could use my assistance in her preparations."

Mrs. Ryan didn't need my assistance any more than she needed a broken leg but a white lie always comes in handy to break off an uncomfortable dialogue. Elder left in the Caddy alone for Deerfield; the day had warmed since its arrival and I was mean-minded enough to exult that dirty slush was going to deface its pristine beauty. I was going to have to squelch my spiteful thoughts lest they surface verbally and inopportunely. My every contact with Elder set my teeth on edge and brought out the worst in me.

Upon Elder's return from Mallory's, he announced that he and Mr. Mallory had decided to have the cremains ready for a memorial service at 2 P.M., next week Thursday. He trusted I would find his choice of the urn satisfactory; the sarcasm was carefully veiled but undeniable. I assured him I trusted his taste and the chosen day and time were entirely acceptable. Then, pleading commitments in the city in the next few days, Elder announced he and Mr. Gordon would depart tomorrow morning for their office. We were to expect them back on Wednesday next. Elder planned to read the will after the memorial service and reception on Thursday. He asked me to assure the presence of Pierce, Mrs. Ryan, the Reverend MacLinn, "and yourself, of course," for the reading. Dinner that evening took place over tasty viands served and eaten in an atmosphere of icy politeness. Elder mostly sat silent, ate, and glowered. He was thoroughly dissatisfied with my attitude—not sufficiently meek, nor docile, nor dutiful, nor grateful for his assiduous attentions. Poor Thomas Gordon tried to keep conversation afloat but we ran into heavy weather once we had exhausted the weather, local landscapes, and the history of Hauteville House as topics. The next morning I donned my well-worn mask of civility and good manners and Elder and I parted with a brief goodbye and a slightly frosty handshake. I was more cordial to Thomas Gordon, saying I hoped he had had a comfortable stay and we would be glad to see him again. He bobbed his head slightly with a sidelong look at his boss; I concluded he was the most junior attorney in at the Elder-Thackeray establishment, his professional fate hanging on every one of the boss's whims.

§ Twenty Three §

THE FOLLOWING WEDNESDAY Mallory brought Papa's ashes back in a simple and tasteful gold-colored container which he placed on the mantle in the drawing room, flanked with handsome bouquets of red carnations and white roses. He brought folding chairs to supplement the seating. The Reverend McLinn and his wife, both white-haired, roly-poly, and soft-voiced, came to check the piano and the best place in the room from which to speak. Thank goodness, the piano was in tune and the dictionary stand from the library made a proper lectern. They departed, pleased with the preparations, planning to return at 1 P.M. the next day for a final check before the service. Elder and Thomas Gordon arrived, laden with luggage in the blue Caddy again, in the late afternoon in time for Elder to pronounce himself satisfied with our efforts. I noticed Mrs. Ryan tighten her lips over clenched teeth when he asked for a copy of her menu for the reception. She handed it to him with the air of an offended duchess, but he was oblivious to his own gaucherie. When he asked me what I proposed to wear, I cut him off with,

"Dear me, Mr. Elder, how unseemly of you. Gentlemen surely leave choice of wardrobe to the ladies. Let me assure you, I and the staff will be properly attired."

He seemed to be abashed and behind his back I saw Thomas Gordon stifle the beginning of a broad smile. Pierce had driven me in to the village where Mrs. Duncan at the dress shop had talked me out of a black faille sheath and into a royal blue velvet gown, long-sleeved, high-necked, full-cut skirt.

"So much more becoming to your coloring, dear, and just as suitable to the occasion. And besides, you can wear it afterwards to other formal and not so formal occasions."

I had to admit as I pivoted in front of the mirror that the color of the fabric favored the blue of my eyes and the soft lines of the skirt swirled gracefully around my calves. Mrs. Duncan recommended I wear a simple necklace with it and I remembered my mother's pearls, lying long unworn in the jewel box on my vanity. Mrs. Duncan also conned me into matching panty hose and classy dark blue suede pumps with one inch heels. When I tried everything on later in the privacy of my bedroom to get the whole effect, I was pleased with the appearance I would make. When I modeled the outfit for Mrs. Ryan and Pierce it met with their unqualified approval. Elegant but understated, so there, Horace Elder!

Everything went off well the next day. Marcus Atwater even came all the way from New York City; he had a hired car and driver and would leave again as soon as the reception was over. I was deeply touched when he wept a few tears as he hugged me in greeting. The Bigelows, the Starks, and the Eisensteins, Bonny, and Ted turned out (Ted in a borrowed sport coat that almost fitted, Jud's I suspected). I insisted that Mr. Mallory seat Mrs. Ryan, Pierce, and the nurses—Mrs. Bettle, Mrs. Wiggs, Arnold—and the maids in the front row of the guests. Mrs. McLinn played old-fashioned hymns softly while the guests were taking their seats. Reverend McLinn delivered a talk somewhere between an eulogy and a sermon. I learned that he had been Papa's first teacher of Greek and Latin, sowing the seeds of scholarship in Papa's boyhood that would grow into Papa's lifelong devotion to classical languages and literature. I also learned that Papa had been confirmed in the Anglican rite and married to my mother in the village church, and that Reverend McLinn had presided over my mother's funeral service. Now, something he said surprised me.

"Armand's life was filled with pain, from the time he lost Felicia and during the years he suffered as an invalid. His pain consumed his life and crowded out the joy he could have taken in his beautiful daughter. Although she stayed faithfully at his side, working with him at his chosen vocation, caring for him without complaint while he lay speechless and motionless, he only rarely displayed the love and affection he carried in his heart. But Armand was conditioned to a profound reserve and was never demonstrative. That he loved his child and doted on her intelligence cannot be doubted. Before he lost the ability to speak, he never failed to tell me proudly of her abilities and achievements. I'm sure that the darkness that fell on him as his infirmity grew more severe did not quench his love and pride; it only inhibited his ability to express it in the usual ways."

Hearing this, I drew a startled breath. Did the Reverend know or guess what Papa had said in that one sentence torn from the depths of his torpor? All those years and only one sentence. "You're a good daughter, Clio." I felt the tears start and hauled out a big linen handkerchief, ever mindful of what salt tears could do to my velvet gown.

The service over, the company repaired to the dining room where Mrs. Ryan and Pierce had laid out a splendid buffet. Mr. Atwater was the only guest who was not known to the others but when I introduced him, he immediately found topics for friendly conversation with each of them. Elder prowled among the guests with a gloomy look on his face, acknowledging them individually with a nod and a mournful smile. He seemed to be attempting the role of chief mourner. I swallowed my antipathy to him and spent my time thanking the others for coming and for their expressions of sympathy. Limiting the number of guests guaranteed a company of kindly neighbors and acquaintances whom I found easy to greet and converse with.

After Pierce had closed the door on the last of the departing guests, the maids went to work clearing away in the dining room, and Elder, Gordon, Pierce, Mrs. Ryan, the Reverend, and I took up places in the morning room. Elder opened his briefcase, extracted a bulky packet of papers, cleared his throat portentously, and began to read.

§ Twenty Four §

Five paragraphs of lawyerese studded with whereases, hereins, and wherefors established Elder as executor of the will of Armand Ladurie DeVille III, and identified me, Clio Felicia DeVille, as the sole offspring of Armand and Felicia DeVille both deceased. Then came, in relatively simple terms, bequests to George Alan Pierce and Wilma Carter Ryan, $5000 cash gifts and annuities of $50,000, large enough (Elder interrupted himself to explain) to provide a significant supplemental income to their Social Security when they chose to retire. Mrs. Ryan, insulted by Elder's condescension, maintained a stone face; Pierce with bent head covered his eyes with his hand while slow tears leaked out over his cheeks. The next bequest was to St Julian's Episcopal Church to fund an endowment of $200,000, eighty percent of the income to be assigned to maintenance or expansion of the fabric of the building and twenty percent to supplement income for the incumbent pastor, whomever he or she might be. Dr. Angus McLinn was cited as an old and dear friend, to whom Armand's personal jewelry (itemized in detail—watch, cuff links, and such) was bequeathed.

A long introduction to the next section of the will explained that a part of Armand III's personal fortune had been inherited from Felicia upon her death, and had been kept *en bloc* to pass to Clio Felicia DeVille as her mother's bequest upon Armand's death. Then came an itemized listing of the securities and bonds encompassed in this maternal bequest, but after Elder had droned his way through a page of them, I entered a plea to dispense with the details and to get on with the rest of the will. Elder screwed up his face in an irritated grimace but acquiesced. He went on to the trust fund being held and managed by the First National Bank of Columbus, the income from which was dedicated to the education of Clio Felicia DeVille. He was about to ramble through that list of holdings but when I cleared my throat rather noisily, he backed off and went on to Papa's residual wealth. This included the Hauteville estate and the House and contents, as well as bonds and securities, the income from which was dedicated to maintenance of the property and expenses of administration. Taken all in all, Papa's bequest to me, Clio Felicia DeVille, added up to about two million in liquid funds and eighteen million in trust or investments, my mother's bloc being some six million of that.

By the time Elder had got that information across, Pierce was sound asleep on his chair, Reverend McLinn was nodding, Mrs. Ryan's mind was far, far away, and I didn't want to hear Elder droning on for what seemed to be four more pages of lists.

"Is that the gist of the will, then?" I asked. "Do we have to hear any more in order to make it legal?"

Thomas Gordon looked up from his reverie with a benign smile, as Elder slapped the papers down on the table.

"I have not completed my entire responsibility as executor, but I have communicated the essentials of the will. If it is your wish to postpone or waive further reading, I must bow to your wishes."

"My wishes are for you to provide me with a complete copy of the will. My personal lawyer will be in touch with you for any of Papa's papers that you may hold. In the meantime, I will expect your office to continue to pay the bills until further notice. In addition, please establish a personal account for me in the amount of $100,000. You may deposit it in the People's Bank and Trust of Fairview."

Elder's mouth dropped open, his face flushed scarlet, and for a minute or so, he was speechless. A kitten had turned into a snarling lion in front of him. He could barely believe his ears. Thomas Gordon shot a sidelong glance at his boss and a calculating look straight at me. Mrs. Ryan jerked her thoughts back from wherever they had been and gazed wide-eyed at the scene. The two old men, alerted by the unspoken tension in the room, woke from their doze and looked around in puzzlement.

"What does this mean?" he sputtered. "You can't dismiss me as executor of your father's will in this cavalier way!"

"I'm not dismissing you as executor of Papa's will. I am expressing my wishes as his legal heir. It's clear to me there is no impediment to your acceding to my express wishes, other than your reluctance to do so."

Elder sputtered some more but I rose and left the room before my resolve dissolved into shaking hands and syncope. Mrs. Ryan and Pierce followed me. We ended up at the table in the servants hall under the curious gaze of the maids and over hastily poured cups of coffee. I regained my composure first and inquired what leftovers from the reception were available for a snack. Mrs. Ryan laughed out loud and even Pierce smiled as he went to explore the refrigerator. I got up refreshed and used the cell phone to call Susan LeMoine; she promised her arrival for tomorrow. As I went through the hall on my way to my room upstairs, I heard muffled conversation in the morning room, Elder's voice sharp, punctuating Gordon's background murmur. Reverend and Mrs. McLinn had let themselves out without a farewell. I would have to call them and apologize for the unpleasantness.

Elder and Gordon took the Caddy and went to the village for their dinner. They returned and stayed the night but the next morning Elder remained in his room, breakfast on a tray, and Gordon informed me he was leaving to go to the office. He would return later in the morning with Papa's papers. I let Bonny know the situation and invited him to be here when Ms. LeMoine arrived. I asked Mrs. Ryan to put out a buffet lunch in the dining room and I told Pierce to reinstate the gong as the signal for meals. I was guessing that the day's events were about to become *ad hoc* occasions.

§ Twenty Five §

I CALLED THE MEETING in the library for 11 A.M. Pierce was sent to summon Elder from his bedroom; Thomas Gordon came in lugging two large cartons stuffed with files; Bonny took up his customary position at the table with his packets of calculator tapes and laptop computer; Ms. LeMoine sat at my desk opposite me, she with her laptop in front of her, me with my computer on and positioned on the blotter. Elder was the last to come in and in order to make his presence indubitably known, sent Pierce for a side table and dining room armchair for his particular use. Pierce complied but the look on his face was one for the books. As soon as everyone was seated, I spoke up to take control of the proceedings. By way of introduction I indicated the tea cart bearing coffee things and a large ice bucket of soft drinks. I went on to say,

"I want to state up front what this meeting is about. First, as Papa's sole heir, I formally request an accounting of his affairs as conducted by Mr. Horace Elder, exercising power of attorney, over the past five to ten years. Second, I require an independent audit of Mr. Elder's management of Papa's financial holdings during the same period. Third, I want an explanation of the disposition of income accruing from the assets held in trust and intended for my 'education,' income of which I have known nothing nor received any part, for an education that was provided in-house, entirely by Papa after the departure of the nannies, tutors, and governesses."

I sat back in my chair, rather pleased that the speech I had rehearsed last night in bed had come off as I had planned. Ms.

LeMoine's fingers had been dancing over the keys as she took notes and she glanced approvingly at me as I continued.

"Perhaps Mr. Elder can address the first of the items on my agenda."

Elder started to his feet, face turkey red, eyes glaring.

"I object strongly to Ms. DeVille's implied accusation. My integrity has never been impugned over the long years I acted with or on behalf of Armand DeVille. I have faithfully reported on an annual basis, every transaction and expenditure I have made involving the DeVille resources. There are, in the files Mr. Gordon has brought, copies of my reports documenting in detail disbursements to household and estate expenses, bank statements for accounts held in the DeVille name, purchases and sales of bonds and securities, communications from the trustees at First National Bank of Columbus, and...and..."

He was running out of steam, words failing him. Thomas Gordon helped him out with a comment. "These boxes hold all the files dealing with DeVille business that I could locate in the office. I am familiar only with those dating from December 1 of this past year, at which time Mr. Elder assigned the DeVille case to me. If Ms. DeVille insists on an independent audit, these files would certainly be adequate to a standard examination. I might add that since I have been working with the DeVille files, I have observed no irregularities."

I was impressed with Gordon's careful phraseology; it gave me some ideas. Were there pertinent files to be found elsewhere than in the office? Were there irregularities possibly to be observed in them prior to December 1 of last year? I noticed Susan LeMoine had picked up on the same nuances. By now Elder was glaring at Gordon, and sputtering: "Mr. Gordon is hardly qualified to open my files to inspection and certainly not to audit by an outsider. His acquaintance with DeVille affairs is a matter of mere months. As my employee, he had no right to raid the documentation I have amassed over years. I sent him this morning to bring back a copy of Armand's will and the data being gathered for the current annual report. He has overstepped his warrant and I will deal with his insubordination in a private interview."

When I looked over at Gordon, I was surprised that he hadn't turned a hair. If he was afraid of Elder's disciplinary action, he wasn't about to show it. His face wore only a bland expression of mild interest. Then he dropped his bombshell.

"As to the trust income designated for Ms. DeVille's education, please note that I have every month deposited it to accounts in her name—half to checking, half to savings—in the Bank of Erie, per Mr. Elder's instructions. The last statements show substantial withdrawals from the savings account. I have the cancelled checks here in this envelope. Perhaps Ms. DeVille has had unusual expenses..."

I exploded. "I have never known of an account or accounts in my name in any bank anywhere, never known of any deposits or withdrawals, never had any money of my own other than what Mrs. Ryan gives me for my small personal expenses. What is this?"

Elder sat stunned, white-faced, deflating like a balloon with a slow leak. Something about those cancelled checks had touched him on the raw. Had he figured out some way to create and loot accounts in my name? A forged signature, perhaps? An accomplice posing as me in transactions with the Bank of Erie? Ms. LeMoine's slender body was as taut as a coiled spring. A smoking gun! the one Bonny suspected but couldn't prove from the records he was reviewing. The tension in the room was overwhelming for everyone except Thomas Gordon, who sat calmly scanning the company with a pleasantly neutral gaze. I was coming to a conclusion that there was a great deal more to Thomas Gordon than met the eye. I hoped Susan LeMoine would look into him as well as Elder. Elder looked so shattered, I felt sorry for him.

"Let's adjourn this meeting and have lunch." I said. "There's a buffet set in the dining room. We can reconvene afterwards for Mr. Elder's explanations."

We rose to leave the room, not looking at Elder, as he shambled out behind us.

§ Twenty Six §

THE BUFFET FEATURED a tureen of lemon rice soup and a generous platter of ham, chicken, tuna, and cheese sandwiches. Another platter bore sticks of carrot and celery, ripe and green olives, sweet and dill pickles, and slices of tomato, colorfully arranged. Bowls of potato chips and corn chips offered salty garnish; a tray of assorted home-baked cookies lay next to the coffee urn. A feast for browsers. Bonny and Gordon ate heartily, Ms. LeMoine concentrated on the vegetable platter, the secret of her figure I was sure, and I was inspired by her example to do the same. Elder ate like a starving man. I knew it was not polite to keep track of a guest's consumption but I wondered; three sandwiches, three bowls of soup, two trips to the chip bowls, and a stack of cookies seemed excessive for a man about to defend his honor in the coming session. And, indeed, his indulgence seemed to cause him a problem as we returned to the library.

I resumed my place behind the desk. Ms. LeMoine, Bonny, and Gordon were shuffling through some files extracted from the cartons. Elder started to sit down on his special chair, but stood up again, announcing to the company,

"I find I am feeling unwell. Please excuse me while I go up to my room to lie down briefly. I will return when this trifling indisposition passes."

He picked up his briefcase and left the room. The rest of us looked at one another, not surprised at all. The size of Elder's lunch as well as the embarrassment caused by Gordon's revelations was good and sufficient reason for him to withdraw temporarily from the battlefield. We all realized his need for privacy to marshal his defense.

Ms. LeMoine came over to me with a manila envelope from which she withdrew several pieces of paper immediately recognizable as checks.

"Are these your signatures?" she asked, arranging five of them on my blotter.

"No, nothing like my handwriting. Here," I pulled out some pages of manuscript from a desk drawer, "this is my writing."

And indeed my careful copperplate was nothing like the back-slanted kindergarten script on the checks. The amounts on the checks were staggering, every one of them was for $500 or more. Each of the five was made out to CASH.

"We'll have to investigate the signature on file with the Bank of Erie," Susan said, "I suspect that the account was opened by a female, the signature put on file genuinely hers, but the name yours. Look, the signatures on the checks show your name in full, 'Clio Felicia DeVille.' That the accomplice is female is quite likely; the handwriting is so neat and quite typical of a girl who learned it at an early age in a public school."

Thomas Gordon decided to add his bit to the conversation,

"On Mr. Elder's trips out of town, he is frequently accompanied by his secretary, Marcia Pate. Office scuttlebutt has it, Ms. Pate is more than a secretary and that the current Mrs. Elder is about to cite her as co-respondent in her divorce action. Now, I don't know anything for sure about that situation but...."

Thomas Gordon's casual leaks of information damning his employer were interesting but suspect—clearly he was deliberately undercutting Elder, hardly admirable behavior for a lawyer on Elder's payroll. It made me wonder what his motives were. Sensing my distrust, he rose and left the room, saying,

"Perhaps I'd better check on Horace. He didn't look so good when he went up to lie down."

He was back in just a few minutes, asking for Dr. Eisenstein's number, saying Horace was having chest pains and trouble breathing. I showed him the hall phone and the doctor's number posted beside it. He spoke with some urgency to Dr. Lev's receptionist. I called off our meeting until Elder's situation had cleared up. By now Bonny and Ms. LeMoine were on a first name basis and she asked me to call her Susan. The two of them were planning strategy and organizing facts to take to the Bank of Erie in order to learn the identity of the ersatz Clio Felicia DeVille. So far, Susan was not recommending application to a judge to depose Elder as executor of Papa's will but she was marshaling the evidence to support that action when it was time to take it. Thomas Gordon just sat by, listening, a neutral expression on his bland visage.

Dr. Lev came soon after and went directly to Elder's room to examine him. He came by the library on his way out to tell us there was no evidence of a cardiac event. He had ordered Hagen to deliver medication to settle the digestive tract and to sedate Elder for a restful sleep. We were to call if there was a recurrence of symptoms. I was glad Mrs. Bettle was still with us so I could give her the job of checking on him. Mrs. Wiggs had left for her daughter's home after the memorial service. Arnold was still convalescing, improving according to Dr. Lev, but not yet fit to travel.

I invited Susan to stay overnight. She accepted with alacrity, saying she kept an overnight case in her car for just such unexpected invitations. Mrs. Ryan set the maids to readying the "peacock" room (named for the wild colors surviving from its art deco past); I thought it highly suitable for a person of Susan's flamboyant style. During our session in the library she had carefully suppressed the flamboyant personality that I knew she possessed, instead maintaining the impassive dignity of an observant attorney. But dinner that evening was pure fun, Bonny stayed over, and the conversation roamed over every topic but today's revelations. Sparkling repartee among Thomas Gordon, Bonny, and Susan had me laughing so hard sometimes I could barely get a fork to my mouth. Susan's wit was no surprise but when Thomas Gordon proved her match, I confess my mixed notions about him underwent some modification. From bland and neutral to witty and urbane was such a change! I wanted very much to like him, if only I could figure out what he was about. Elder's sleeping presence upstairs failed to cast a cloud over our evening. After coffee in the drawing room, Bonny departed and the rest of us retired for the night. My cheerful mood persisted until I fell asleep and even on into my dreams.

§ Twenty Seven §

I was wakened by a soft but rapid rat-a-tat-tat on my door. The display on the bedside clock read 6:30. Shrugging on a robe and shuffling into my slippers, I opened to find Pierce, his face a mask of distress.

"Oh, Miss Clio," he said. "Mr. Elder is dead, dead and cold. I went in to take him his morning coffee and found him. But he's dead, he's really dead...."

"Come on," I said. "Show me."

I towed him behind me into the red room where indeed Elder lay comfortably disposed on his right side, but still and stark, cold to the touch. Protruding from the left side of his back was the brightly enameled haft of a dagger that I recognized as normally a part of the display of Oriental weapons hanging in the hall. Pierce stood behind me, his breathing loud and rasping in his chest. His difficult respiration worried me and I sent him out to rest in the hall while I looked around the room, careful not to touch anything. I came out to find Pierce sitting on the antique chest, head bent, arms wrapped tightly around his chest.

"Are you all right?" I questioned.

He nodded and rose, shaking himself into his usual shoulders-back, head-up posture. His breathing had steadied and quieted. So I sent him to tell Mrs. Ryan, who was already up and preparing for breakfast, and went down to phone the Sheriff's office. It took repetition to get through to the sleepy dispatcher that murder was the topic of my call, but once awake, she asked all the right questions, then cautioned against touching anything at the murder scene, said a unit would be along within 20 minutes, and. instructed me to detain anyone already in the house from leaving before the deputies arrived.

I went down to the kitchen where Mrs. Ryan sat wringing her hands at the table, her breakfast preparations on hold. As I entered, Mrs. Bettle toddled in, dressed in robe and slippers, looking for a cup of coffee before going to check on her patient.

"He should still be asleep, Dr. Lev's opiate was a strong one. My goodness, what's the matter? Your faces are as long as a rainy Monday. What's wrong?"

She did not take the explanation well; she insisted on going to the red bedroom to assure herself that her patient was dead. I went along to assure that her investigation did not disturb the scene. She felt for pulses in wrist and neck, agreed the body was cold, and stood back unhappily, saying,

"I checked him at midnight, opened the window a few inches and pulled aside the drapes, and he was sleeping like a baby. I was planning to check on him again at 7 A.M. This is awful, who could have done this? It's murder, that's what it is. That knife, or whatever it is, points right between two ribs and into his heart."

I drew her away from the room, suggesting that she and I both should get dressed to receive the officers who were on the way.

Soon the circle drive in front of the house was populated by four sheriff's cars, Jud Bigelow's among them. The Sheriff himself headed the delegation: a forensic specialist with a lapel tape recorder and a large black briefcase, two detectives with notebooks, a rookie with a lapel radio, staying close on the Sheriff's heels—and Jud, apparently along because it was his district where the crime had occurred. Pierce escorted the Sheriff and his crew to the red bedroom, then went to rouse Thomas Gordon, Susan LeMoine, and Arnold Slocum and summon them to the table in the servants hall. Mrs. Bettle was already in attendance and Mrs. Ryan had recovered her poise sufficiently to set out bread for toast, butter and jam, and to fire up the 30-cup coffee urn. When Pierce and I joined the group in the kitchen the questions flew thick and fast. I imposed a sort of order on them by asking Mrs. Bettle to tell her story first, Pierce next, and I last. Susan, Gordon, and Arnold had nothing to contribute in the way of information, each saying they had retired between 9 and 10 P.M., Gordon to read for an hour, Susan to go over some papers in her briefcase, Arnold to watch TV. Each had slept soundly, undisturbed thereafter. When Mrs. Ryan rose to call the maids and tell them to delay their arrival until 1 o'clock, Susan broached the sore point lurking in everyone's mind.

"You all know—the timing and nature of Elder's death point to a murderer in the house between midnight when Mrs. Bettle found him alive and well and 6:30 when Pierce found him stabbed to death. That casts suspicion on every one of the guests and staff except for the maids. In my capacity as Clio's legal counsel, I urge every one of you to respond truthfully to every question the law officers pose to you. There's an old saw, 'the truth shall set you free' and it's as true as truth itself. If any one of you feel the need for a lawyer before you respond to any questions, I know of four in the village capable of advising you."

The cautions were sobering, but no one flinched as Susan and I looked around. Arnold took another piece of toast and crunched it noisily; Pierce and Mrs. Ryan glared their disapproval of his bad manners. Mrs. Bettle blew her nose also noisily, while Gordon looked on with his customary bland expression and poured himself another cup of coffee. The tension was redirected when one of the detectives entered, accompanied by Jud, who introduced him as Sergeant Bu An Ky. Sergeant Ky lost no time starting the questions. Beginning with me, he asked each of us to account for all of our time and every encounter with Elder between mid-afternoon of yesterday and this morning. He quickly established that Mrs. Bettle had seen Elder alive at two-hour intervals between 5 P.M. and midnight; and that she had given him Dr. Lev's medication at 5 P.M. when Pierce had filled the bedside carafe with fresh water. He interrupted our respective timetables with questions like: Did you leave your room or see or hear anyone moving about the house after retiring or after midnight? (No one had although the question made Arnold nervous.) Did you know what the murder weapon was? (Everyone did, the table conversation had seen to that.) Describe it, please. Mrs. Ryan, Pierce, and I could do so quite well, we had each dusted the weapons trophy for years. Arnold admitted some passing awareness of it since he had been in the house. Gordon and Susan had noticed the trophy but not individual items in it. Mrs. Bettle had never paid attention to the trophy or any of its components and couldn't see why anyone would want to look at that old stuff. Then Detective Ky asked to use the morning room for individual interviews. Jud was to sit in on the interviews. Mrs. Ryan was first and soon released, relieved to get back to managing the meals. Pierce was next; he left the morning room, his face white and his hands shaking, telling us Ky had grilled him about the carafe and his discovery of the body. He was really shaken up and Mrs. Ryan immediately set him to setting the table for lunch by way of distraction. Mrs. Bettle flounced out next, indignant over what she perceived as criticism of her professional behavior, grumbling "no sense at all to check every two hours after midnight on a man deep asleep," (she almost said dead to the world but caught herself in time) and "vital signs perfectly normal at 5 P.M." Arnold emerged from the question session sweating but calm, pleaded flu aftermath, and retired to his room.

§ Twenty Eight §

Sheriff Land and Ky did the next round of interviews; Jud was dismissed to other duties. Susan's session with the sheriff was short and she seemed to have suffered no stress from it. Thinking as she did that truth was priority one, I did wonder if she thought "*all* the truth" was included in that priority. I wondered the same of Thomas Gordon, who spent a good half hour with Sheriff Land, and who emerged from the morning room as coolly bland and even jauntier than he had gone in. Then it was my turn.

Land rose to greet me, hand outstretched to shake mine.

"Ms. DeVille. Not having met you before, I wish the circumstances were happier, but I am nevertheless pleased to make your acquaintance."

The Sheriff was a big man, tall and portly, made to appear even bigger by his garb—broad leather belt and Sam Brown, holster with big gun, insignia-studded epaulets on his dark brown serge uniform. He had the weather-beaten face of an outdoorsman, sleepy grey eyes, crew-cut gray hair, and a kind of hail-fellow-well-met expression—and a disarming manner, a clear advantage in conducting crime scene interviews.

I responded by asking him if he had found the household staff helpful in facilitating his investigation and he assured me he had no complaints.

"Now, Ms. DeVille, I'm going to ask you to tell us again what you did and where you were between yesterday noon and 6:30 this morning."

Sergeant Ky's ballpoint pen started to fly over the pages of his notebook. I obliged with essentially the same tale I had given Ky earlier and waited for the next inquiry.

"Why was Horace Elder staying overnight? I understand Mr. Armand DeVille's will had been read the previous day. One would think Mr. Elder's business here was more or less complete...."

"He was staying because he and I had differences of opinion about his management of my father's resources in the past. Since he was designated executor of my father's will, I wanted him to answer some serious questions about the legacy. I asked for papers belonging to my father that had to be brought from the offices of the Elder-Thackeray firm. Mr. Gordon went to get them and I then met with Mr. Elder, Mr. Gordon, Ms. LeMoine, and Mr. Harvill yesterday morning. After lunch, Mr. Elder felt unwell and retired to his bedroom; we called Dr. Eisenstein who examined him and prescribed medication and regular monitoring by Mrs. Bettle. The doctor assured us Mr. Elder's condition was nothing serious."

"Would you specify your differences in detail and indicate how serious they were? I should tell you, Mr. Gordon has provided quite a thorough description of the morning meeting and Ms. LeMoine, within the limits of the confidentiality owed to a client, has done so as well."

I recounted as best I could recall the exchanges between myself and Elder. Prompted by Land, I also recounted the conversation Gordon, Susan, Bonny, and I had in the afternoon after Elder had left us.

"So the exchanges were heated, and the charges you raised were serious. I understand from Ms. LeMoine, you were planning to seek removal of Mr. Elder as executor of your father's will and were even considering legal action against him. Now I hope you will not be insulted by my mental processes, but might we not think of revenge as a motive for murder? Or murder as an alternative to a long and costly court battle?"

His words were like a jolt of electricity. I lost my cool, the words of my reply came in a loud and high-pitched tone.

"I freely admit I disliked Horace Elder intensely. I freely admit I was planning to go after him with all my energy and resources to nullify his control of my inheritance. But, so help me God, as much as I wanted him to pay for the wrongs he had done to the DeVilles, and as much as I wanted him to be out and clear of the DeVille affairs, I DID NOT EVEN THINK of murder as a solution. I grant your suspicion of me can be justified, I knew of the means, I had opportunity and an apparent motive, but I DID NOT do the deed. I could not even imagine murder as a solution to my relationship with Horace Elder."

I sat back in my chair, breathing hard and shaking with my emotions. Too much had happened in my world in the last two weeks—bottled up tensions, mourning still fresh, new worries added to old, all of it seemed to have culminated in one outburst. Sheriff Land sat there, his face noncommittal, patiently waiting until I was calm again.

"I'm sorry," I said. "My outburst was rude and over reactive. But let me repeat, I never had intent nor did I ever act to do physical harm to Horace Elder."

Then he took me completely by surprise when he asked,

"What do you know of Arnold Slocum?

"Arnold? What should I know? He was hired through the Home Medical Agency. We have always relied on the background checks of personnel they supply and we have always found their people competent and qualified."

"He was the attendant, was he not, on the shift before the incident of your father's damaging seizure? And you were the attendant when that seizure occurred, were you not?"

"Of course. Dr. Lev—Dr. Eisenstein that is—was looking into the potency and efficacy of the medication which failed to control that seizure. Why are you asking questions about the event? I suggest you check with Dr. Eisenstein, he should have the drug company's findings by now."

"Well, we will be checking with Dr. Lev and also looking further into Mr. Slocum's history. By the way, do we have your permission to search the house or will I be obliged to get a warrant?"

Another jolt! "Why a search? Wasn't the murder weapon found in the body?" I was dumbfounded by his reply.

"Of course, we have no need to search for the murder weapon. However, there's a question of drugs in the house. We cannot avoid pursuing them. Now, I think that's enough for the moment. We'll undoubtedly have more questions as our investigation progresses."

I set my jaw stubbornly, a search was an invasion of privacy I was not prepared to tolerate. But I couldn't rationalize withholding permission, and so I gave it in kind of a fog. Of course, there were drugs in the house, or had been—Papa's medications, the medications delivered for Elder's indisposition and those prescribed for Arnold's flu, Mrs. Ryan took something for her high blood pressure; and I was sure we all had over-the-counter stuff in our bathroom medicine cabinets. I asked Land to delay the search until the staff had been informed and then to let me and Susan to be present while it proceeded. When he gave me a sharp look of inquiry, I told him I was unwilling to violate the privacy of staff and guests without some safeguard. He bowed to my wishes but insisted that he and I instruct everyone to stay out of their quarters until further notice. Gordon and Susan were in the library; and Mrs. Ryan, Pierce, and Mrs. Bettle were in the kitchen. Each of them took my announcement in good part. Arnold was in his room, TV blaring, and got no advance notice.

§ TWENTY NINE §

THE "PEACOCK" ROOM, Susan's bedroom, and its adjoining bath was first on the agenda. The search was quick, efficient, neat, and fruitless. Until Susan had spent an overnight in the room, years had passed since the last occupant. Drawers, cabinets, closets were empty—Mrs. Ryan did not tolerate such unused spaces being used for storage. Thomas Gordon's room and bath underwent the same kind of search, although there were a few more personal items, spare shirts, underwear, socks, to be examined. On to Mrs. Bettle's room, warm and cozy as a mouse's nest, knickknacks on every flat surface—she had lived in it for some fifteen years and made it very much her own. The search was as thorough here as elsewhere but in no way as quick; I suspected she had indulged her pack rat genes and squirreled away every birthday card and magazine she had ever received. The search here was also fruitless except for a bottle of aspirin, a box of liniment wraps, and a large bottle of Kao-Pectate. Mrs. Ryan's room yielded not much more, although the prescription number on her vial of blood pressure medication got close scrutiny and a jotting in Ky's notebook. Her cabinets, drawers, and closets were as Spartan in their contents and as neatly arranged as her severe coiffure. Pierce's room was rather chaotic, coats, shirts, and pants neatly hung but closet floors cluttered with shoes, boxes, paper bags, bureau drawers tumbled with socks and underwear any which way. An untidy pile of magazines lay next to his easy chair. I was seeing a side of Pierce I would never have imagined. His working appearance was all spit and polish, brushed and combed, but the brushes on top of his bureau were clogged with white hairs and the silver-backed comb was black with tarnish. His collection of pharmacy items was more extensive than anyone's but ran the gamut only from Visine to analgesics (five kinds, among them aspirin and ibuprofen). Pierce never complained of aches and pains but he must be having them.

The knock on Arnold's door had to be loud and prolonged, his TV was blaring so loudly. He opened it and stared bleary-eyed at the crowd waiting in the hall. The sheriff announced his and the Sergeant's intention to search the room, I added that I had given permission and Ms. LeMoine was present as a witness. Faced with all this official notice, Arnold went pale as a ghost and crouched warily on a chair next to the window. I wrinkled my nose, there was a funny smell in the room. "Marijuana" Susan breathed in my ear. I heard Sergeant Ky say, "Roll up your sleeves, please," followed by Arnold's weak protest and eventual obedience. Just then, the sheriff held up a plastic bag of something that looked like birdseed. More jottings in the notebook. The room was too dark for me to see what Ky had spotted on Arnold's arms, but I heard Susan whisper, "Needle marks." From a shelf in the closet, the sheriff pulled a box labeled with the name and colored logo of the medication that had rescued Papa from his seizures. The box was full of unopened, opened, and partially depleted vials, and used syringes and needles. I gasped in shock.

"Ms. Clio," the sheriff said. "This is now a criminal investigation of Arnold Slocum for the use and possession of a controlled substance. Since there is no longer a question of invasion of privacy, you and Ms. LeMoine need not stay as we continue the search and make our arrest."

I opened my mouth to say something, but Susan tugged on my elbow and drew me out of the room. "We're out of it now, let's leave it to the cops," she hissed. I could hear Sergeant Ky beginning the Miranda warning, and a *non sequitur* ran through my mind, hadn't the Supreme Court changed that? Then Susan tugged me along the hall and down the stair to the library, where Thomas Gordon was still poring over a stack of papers.

"Guess what?" Susan burst out.

§ THIRTY §

GORDON ROSE, INTEREST replacing his usually noncommittal expression and putting a sparkle in his eyes. Susan launched into a full description of our observations during the search of the rooms, ending triumphantly with the disclosure of Arnold's transgressions. Gordon nodded and began,

"Well, well, well. Very interesting, adds some spice to a pot that didn't need any more. Miss Clio.... "

I interrupted, unintentionally waspish, "Just Clio, I'm tired of all this formality. You can be Thomas."

He came back with "Tom! please! I hate Thomas, reminds me of my childhood and an aunt who thought Thomas Too Too Twain was a cute name for her 4-year old nephew. But to get back to what I was going to say—I hope, Clio, you aren't banking on Arnold's druggy doings getting you off the hook. After all, you can still be suspected of doctoring medication or withholding it to bring about your father's death, and of slipping that fancy shiv into Horace's back. What I mean is—nothing arising from discovery of Arnold's misdeeds dispels the cloud of suspicion that hangs over your head. As it happens, and if contributes to your peace of mind, Susan and I have put our heads together and decided you aren't the murdering type...."

"Thanks a bunch!" I retorted. "Thanks for your faith in me! I'll write this down in my diary...." My voice failed, choked on my sarcasm.

"Hold your horses. It's not just faith, We reviewed circumstances and a couple of clues we wormed out of your friend Jud and concluded that suspicion doesn't hold up. First of all, although you had opportunity for years and years to do in your father, there's never been an untoward incident. We checked with Mrs. Bettle, discreetly of course. Secondly, we were witness to your intent for a legal revenge against Horace and the passion you displayed to pursue it. People who plan to follow up on an as yet unproved financial injury in the courts are unlikely to rely on murder to get even. It's hard enough to get money back from a live scoundrel and nearly impossible to get it from a dead one. Thirdly, we like you, maybe that's where some faith comes in."

This time I said thanks with tears in my eyes. Then, I said, "What clues?"

It seems Jud had let slip that the carafe in Horace's room had tested positive for a barbiturate but Horace had no sleeping medication among his possessions, nor had Dr. Lev prescribed anything of the sort for Elder's indigestion. The carafe and contents were going for analysis, definitive results due in a few days. Another nebulous clue was the angle of penetration of the dagger, which was compatible with a right-handed reach *across* Horace's body, a reach that seemed to indicate attack by a taller, longer-armed person than I. None of the clues excluded me from suspicion in the eyes of Sheriff Land and his henchmen but they were enough to back up the faith Tom and Susan professed.

As these scraps of information came out, I began to sense an understanding between Tom and Susan that went beyond their words, a kind of complicity, so to speak. They kept throwing quick glances at one another, then at me, as if their telepathic connection was asking, shall we or shall we not. I took the bull by the horns,

"OK, you two. What do you know that you're keeping from me? If you believe in my innocence, there's no reason I can't know everything you do."

Tom grinned at Susan, "Didn't I tell you she'd catch on? Now, hear this," he said to me.

"I am a fully qualified attorney, Clio; I work for the state Attorney

General. I was planted undercover in the Elder-Thackeray law firm as of last December by the A-G. I've been a mole, a spy. I got the DeVille files when Horace assigned their administration to me, along with responsibility for several other clients' affairs. He probably thought as a newcomer to the firm, I wouldn't be able to spot hanky panky. You know the proverb about pride going before the fall, Well, smug and arrogant pretty well describes Horace's personality, don't you think? Actually, my mission for the A-G was to investigate from the inside the mishandling of matters confided to Elder-Thackeray by several very influential cronies of the governor. By the way, Thackeray bought out his partnership nine years ago, leaving only his name associated with the firm. Whatever misdeeds have occurred, they can be charged up to Horace and two accomplices, junior partners too junior to have their names on the door. Now, the way things have turned out, my job will be to take back these boxes of DeVille documents to the Elder-Thackeray office, inform the estranged latest Mrs. Elder and the unfortunate Marcia Pate of Horace's death, and entertain a swarm of IRS and FBI agents and the A-G's crew of investigators and auditors, as they go through the firm with a fine tooth comb. The DeVille problems will be only a part of the investigation, and a small one at that. Susan and I have already agreed to file a joint petition on your behalf with Judge Abercrombie to appoint an executor of Mr. DeVille's will and an administrator of the estate. Are you understanding what I'm saying? Are you OK? You've gone white."

I seemed to be looking down an endless dark tunnel, hearing, as if from a great distance,

"Catch her, she's going...."

When I woke up I was stretched on the leather divan in front of the fireplace, gas log blazing, an afghan tucked snugly around me, and a crowd hovering near. Mrs. Ryan was holding a thermos of some hot fluid, Pierce a mug, saucer, and napkin, and Tom and Bonny (who must have arrived while I was visiting the dark place) were lifting my head and shoulders onto cushions, apparently preparatory to pouring liquids into me. Susan was saying "She's had no lunch, she needs food. It's 2:30 and she's had nothing since breakfast."

I was still woozy but after a cup of Mrs. Ryan's chicken broth, I felt well enough to wobble down to the servants hall to eat, Mrs. Ryan and Pierce preceding, the others following to ensure my safe passage. After a bowl of tomato bisque and a hastily cobbled egg salad sandwich, I felt fully recuperated. A good thing, too. The next phase of law and order was about to begin.

Sheriff Land appeared, accompanied by a white-coated, crew-cut fellow carrying a briefcase.

"Ah, great, everyone's here," Land said, "Lieutenant Allerd needs to get fingerprints."

So, each of us, hands cleaned with waterless wash, fingers inked up and pressed on cards neatly lettered with our names, de-inked with waterless wipes, became a candidate for AFIS searches and in-house matches. We had just been dismissed from the fingerprinting event when a slight scuffle in the upstairs hall drew our attention. The scuffle proved to be the rather uncooperative departure of Arnold for the Huron County lockup, cuffed and flanked by Sergeant Ky and Jud Bigelow. The next entry in the parade to the front door was the coroner's crew, coming down the stair from the red bedroom, with the gurney bearing a silvery vinyl body bag enclosing the bulky outline of Horace Elder, and followed by Lieutenant Allerd and his briefcase. We all stood respectfully to let it pass. Bonny, Susan, and Tom returned to the library to finish boxing up Elder-Thackeray documents and to returning DeVille documents to the filing cabinet. Bonny was stuffing his tote bag with his computer, calculator, notebooks, and neatly packaged printout strips.

"Tom tells me," Bonny explained, "my work for you must go on hold until the legal situation is sorted out and areas of responsibility are defined. I'm still your employee, just on leave for a while, hopefully not very long. "

I nodded, watching them until voices in the hall caught my

attention. Dr. Lev and Sheriff Land were in animated conversation with Mrs. Bettle on the second-floor landing. Most of the animation came from Mrs. Bettle, sobbing and blaming herself tearfully for lax maintenance of the medication inventory in Papa's treatment record.

She moaned between sobs, "My fault, all my fault. I should have kept better track when medication was delivered. I logged or verified every bit that was used, but somewhere along the line, things just got away from me."

Dr. Lev was leafing one last time through the log book before handing it over to the sheriff. Then he patted Mrs. Bettle on the back, told her to stop crying, and sent her off to her room to recover. As he and the sheriff were passing through the hall on their way out, he came over and put his arm around me,

"I want you to tuck yourself up for a nice long sleep as soon as all these strangers clear out. You seem to me to be about used up. You hear me?"

I nodded. Following his instructions sounded like the most desirable prospect I had ever heard. Then Tom and Susan came down with their luggage, they and Bonny carried out their boxes and bags of documents, and I bid them all farewell from the front steps. Pierce closed the front door behind them with an air of finality and I went to follow Dr. Lev's orders. Drunk on hot chocolate furnished by Mrs. Ryan, relaxed by a long hot soak in the bathtub, I climbed into my favorite flannel pajamas and fell into bed and dreamless sleep.

§ Thirty One §

I WOKE THE NEXT morning refreshed in body, but my brain churning over the happenings of the preceding day. My thoughts were no more organized after two cups of coffee so I put on parka and boots and went for a walk in the woods. The weather was bright and cold; old snow still lay white and drifted under the bushes and trees although the lane to the back of the property was reasonably clear. Walter Stark must have plowed it out when he heard of the goings on at the House. I blessed him for a clear path for my walk. Off to the side, as I passed the dilapidated groundskeeper's cottage, a cardinal flashed like red lightning over the white clearing, followed by the noisy blue whirlwind of a jay. Rabbits had been out and about, their triple paw prints crisscrossing the snowscape. I stopped to muse, remembering the spring day that I had rushed over to confront Ted roasting his rabbit in the fireplace. I had to recognize that day as a turning point in my life. So much had happened since. As I stood there—motionless, running over in my mind all the events that had shaken up my sterile routine of watch-on-watch at Papa's bedside, interspersed with stints at my translation desk, meals, and bed—a vixen crept cautiously, belly low over the snow, from behind a tree and leapt in a flurry on some hapless prey. She straightened and tensed as she spotted me, the tail of a mouse dangling from her mouth, then she scampered away to notify her kits that dinner was served. Realizing my feet were freezing, I pivoted to return to the house, grateful for the glimpses of the ancient drama of life that wild creatures played every day. Maybe today was another turning point in my life.

I was ready for a hearty breakfast and Mrs. Ryan obliged with ham and eggs, toast and orange wedges. As I rose from the table, wiping my mouth with my napkin, I heard Pierce at the front door as he admitted visitors, by their voices male. They proved to be Sergeant Ky and Lieutenant Allerd, announcing their intent to spend more time in the red bedroom and Arnold's room. I gave them the run of the house but warned them that the maids were scheduled to clean the downstairs rooms and my bedroom. No problem, they were not interested in any of those locations. I told them they could look at the staff rooms again, providing they obtained permission from the occupants first. Thanking me politely, they went cheerfully up the stair to their work. I recalled that my reference books and translations-in-progress needed to be put in order before I could settle down to constructive work again, and headed for the library.

Pierce called me for lunch at 11:30 and I went down to find the policemen had been invited to share it. Conversation was general but devoid of reference to current events. The lieutenant displayed a pretty turn of wit as he bantered with Lily (Roseanne's little sister); she was a pretty thing herself and something of a flirt. Ky was very formal, responding only when addressed. I held my breath when Clara, the other maid, asked Ky if he was Chinese. We didn't need any racist *faux pas* in the house at this time. But Ky took it in good part; no, he said, he was American but his parents were Viet Namese.

"Hey, wow!" Clara burst out brightly. "My dad was a soldier in Viet Nam, he hated the war but he loved the people. He still writes to a teacher who lives in Hue; they got to be friends when dad was stationed at Da Nang. We'd like to go visit sometime."

Ky smiled pleasantly and continued eating his tuna fish salad. Mrs. Ryan cut conversation short when she decided it was time for the girls to get back to their work and sent them off. They were nice kids, fresh-faced, wholesome, just out of high school, Lily working to get tuition money for beauty school, Clara working to supplement the family income (mom stay-at-home to look after four little kids, making do on a disabled veteran's pension, dad a paraplegic).

I had risen to go back to the library when Pierce came to announce Ms. Susan was on the phone for me.

"Clio," she began, "Tom and I got together with Judge Abercrombie this morning. Considering the complications, we thought we needed to explain the situation before presenting our petition. He was so willing to entertain the petition that he had us write it out by hand right then and there. We learned that Armand DeVille had been his classmate at Harvard and what's more, the judge had had a strong suspicion of Elder's shenanigans for at least the past two years. To get to the nitty-gritty of this call—the judge proposed appointing Carter Evans as executor and administrator of the DeVille estate. But he wanted you to meet him and find the appointment agreeable before it was certified."

"I never heard of a Carter Evans. How will I know that Abercrombie has any better judgment than Horace Elder? Elder was Papa's classmate, too. I'm beginning to think the old boy network was Papa's only connection with the outside world, and not a very reliable one at that."

"Well, Carter Evans is a legendary legal figure. He's retired from a federal judgeship which he accepted after a stellar career as a litigator—highly qualified to make his way through the ins and outs of the DeVille estate. He's a former special envoy to Greece and served a stint as counsel to the president, has been investigated by the CIA and FBI, and given top security clearances. Integrity is his middle name. He's teaching some law school classes now and confesses to being bored. If you like him when you meet him, he would be available immediately."

Susan paused for breath; in the background I could hear Placido Domingo belting out an aria. She must be calling from her car. I took a minute to think. The kind of praise heaped on Carter Evans by a practicing skeptic like Susan was a recommendation in itself. I finally replied.

"All right, set up a meeting with him. Would he come here or will he insist I come to him? Where does he live, incidentally?"

Susan didn't know but she would get back to me when she had made arrangements. I hung up the phone with a sigh. I had met more strangers in the last year than I had in the past fifteen years. I wasn't sure I liked that. It seemed to complicate things beyond my capacity to bear them.

Susan called back the next day and said Carter Evans thought it best if he met me on my own turf, if I was amenable. I was and set it up for lunch on Thursday. I told Mrs. Ryan and Pierce to make the preparations and that I planned to introduce him to them. If he ended up holding the purse strings for the household, I wanted their approval of the man. The two of them nodded solemnly and started hauling out fancy linens, silver, china, crystal—I was beginning to believe they liked having guests. Maybe the bustle made them feel young again. Pierce had always told stories of Armand and Felicia, newlyweds, their frequent parties and numerous guests; I think Mrs. Ryan had heard and absorbed his stories so often that she remembered them as events she had lived. In any case, the menu she brought for me to OK was quite splendid—clear jellied consommé, crusty cornbread sticks, roast Cornish game hen, wild rice pilaf, asparagus spears, and flan with cinnamon cream. Describing it, she bemoaned the dilapidation of the conservatory—in the old days at this season of the year, she said, fresh asparagus would have been up and ready for the plucking out there, and flowers for the table too. With a sideways glance at me, she wondered wistfully whether some of the old amenities would be condoned by a new administrator. Horace Elder always poor-mouthed suggestions for replacing shabby furnishings, keeping up the conservatory, or tidying the grounds. I just shrugged and said the menu was very nice, go with it. But after she left, I let my mind wander and did a bit of dreaming myself—my own car (although I'd have to take driving lessons), a hi-fi system for good music (although hi-fi was a hopelessly outmoded term for it), trips to New York or Chicago to visit museums or to see plays (although I could wish for a companion to share them with). There must be plenty of money for some of these things, but then I shook myself and remembered the foolishness of counting one's chickens before they're hatched. It would be a good while before anyone actually knew whether and how much money there was for the things we fancied. I hope that this superlative lawyer who was on his way would live up to his billing.

Well, Thursday came, and so did Carter Evans. My mental picture of him had been an avuncular septuagenarian, limping along with a silver-headed cane, so I was really taken aback when he proved to be tall, athletic, and although silver-haired, apparently not much past his fifties. Pierce had shown him into the drawing room and he rose with a courtly bow as I entered. His face was pleasantly ordinary, rather bony, set with bright hazel eyes; his handshake was warm and firm, but not domineering; his smile was genuine and disclosed excellent teeth. His appearance and manner made an excellent first impression. Not only on me. Pierce lurked at the door prior to offering sherry; approval was stamped all over his face, this was a *gentleman*! Mr. Evans accepted sherry, complimented us on its excellence, sat down, and sipped it gracefully. Evans's elegant manners not only impressed me, they made me glad I had worn my beautiful blue funeral dress and my mother's pearls. I hoped he was as impressed by my appearance as I was with his. Unfortunately, I was short of small talk and we soon ran out of commentary on the weather and newspaper headlines. Then, bless the man, he undertook to rescue me from the conversational doldrums with queries about my latest translations. He related his experience while in Greece, seeing plays by Aeschylus in the very theaters where they had premiered.

"You know, I was selected for the special envoy's job there primarily because of my reputation as a Greek scholar. That reputation is somewhat over-rated, I'm woefully out of practice since most of my work dates back some twenty-five years. I would love to see some of yours provided you are kind enough not to stress my memory."

"How did you hear of my work with Greek plays? I certainly have not a reputation in the scholarly world as my father had."

"Marcus Atwater. He literally bubbles with enthusiasm when he speaks of your latest efforts. You look puzzled—and well you might, but Marcus and I have lunch the first Saturday of every month and have for years whenever I'm in the country. I heard of you before you heard of me."

Just then Pierce sounded the gong for lunch and we proceeded to the dining room. Before we sat down, I introduced Pierce and Mrs. Ryan to Evans in formal terms and let him know I had invited them to join us for coffee and dessert. He raised one eyebrow but furled it immediately when I told him that they managed the household finances and had been my best friends through all the trying times of Papa's illness. Without further ado, he reached to shake hands with each of them, with a friendly smile and gracious words of greeting. Lunch went off very nicely and with the service of the flan and coffee, Pierce and Mrs. Ryan joined us at the table. Pierce seemed a bit nervous, in his mind, a butler didn't presume to sit down at the same table as his employer (he obviously forgot that he and I sat at the same table in the servants hall for most of our meals and had done so for years). Mrs. Ryan, on the other hand, was completely at ease, having been mistress of her domain for so many years.

§ Thirty Two §

CARTER EVANS MADE it easy for us. He began with an abbreviated bio, not puffing his accomplishments, just laying them out as matters of fact. He had been more than Papa's classmate, had in fact, shared a dorm unit with him for two years at Harvard and been a member of the Cosmos Club as well. He joined his uncle's law firm in New York City upon graduation and practiced there for several years, leaving only to attend the Wharton School for an MBA, the better to serve the firm's business clients. He was then contacted by the State Department and asked to shepherd some overseas litigation about marine rights through the International Court in the Hague; the next step in his career was an appointment as special envoy to Greece, charged with ironing out a complicated trade dispute. He had married a childhood sweetheart in his twenties but as his career took him abroad often and for long periods, his wife, who hated living abroad, faced him with a choice between her and his career; they agreed first to separate and then to divorce. They had had no children and the divorce was amicable. He returned from Greece at the request of the President and worked in the White House for a time, and was then offered a Federal judgeship. His account of all the FBI and CIA investigations and the Congressional committee inquiries was interesting and occasionally amusing, but he made it clear his personal and professional reputation had emerged enhanced by the rigor of the procedures. He said he had enjoyed the Federal bench but had eventually tired of the work loads. Retiring allowed him to teach and also to have plenty of time for private clients. When he finished, he looked up with a smile and a chuckle,

"You may have heard more of me than you wished, but that's the way it is. Susan told me generally of your current situation. It sounded like an interesting challenge. In case you wonder as to my qualifications for administration, I maintain a highly competent staff with sterling credentials, since I also serve as administrator for several other estates. My fees are modest, just enough to cover expenses; I have independent means, some inherited, some from investment income, some from sales of my law texts. If you would like to have all this on paper, I have a *curriculum vitae* and bibliography out in the car, and will give it to you whenever you want it. I'll be happy to answer any questions."

Mrs. Ryan rose and took out her household ledger from a drawer of the sideboard. She spread it open in front of Evans and asked,

"These are the household expenses for Hauteville House. Please look at them and tell me whether you think them reasonable for day-to-day operations. I can't give you chapter and verse for all the expenses since many of them were billed directly to Horace Elder's office—electricity, fuel, roof repairs, and such."

Evans pulled a pair of half glasses out of his breast pocket and read and leafed, asked an occasional question, and finally looked up with one more question,

"And you have managed this household—salaries for nurses and staff, 'Miss Clio's petty cash,' groceries, Mr. Armand's medication, minor repairs—on the monthly allowance shown here?"

Mrs. Ryan hastened to say, almost apologetically,

"Of course, the expenses will be significantly less when I'm not paying salaries for nurses and a big pharmacy bill. I will still have to keep the maids to do cleaning and laundry—this is a big house, as you can see, although, during Mr. Armand's illness, we have controlled expenses by closing unused areas."

"You are to be complimented on your frugal management.

Similar households have expenses three times these, even aside from medical expenses. Your expenditure for nurses alone is very small considering the amount of care Mr. Armand must have required. You seem to be not only housekeeper but cook—and a very good one I must say—and Pierce is butler, chauffeur, and Mr. Armand's valet. This is a huge house and what I've seen of it is beautifully kept. You have managed very efficiently with only limited hours and dollars to spend on the services of maids."

"I fill in on handyman's chores, too," Pierce inserted.

"Mrs. Ryan, how much more money do you think would be appropriate to add to the household budget?" Evans asked.

Mrs. Ryan blushed and stumbled over her reply,

"I really can't say. It's probably presumptuous for me to make suggestions. But there should be more money for Miss Clio's clothes and books, and for entertainment—a TV that would play those movie discs or tapes, a music system too. When she wasn't sitting with Mr. Armand, she spent all her time working in the library, never went out for fun. Now that she doesn't have to look after her father, she needs to balance her work with something recreational; working all the time is not good for her. Although the events of the past weeks have brought her some new friends and given us all some excitement. We've had plenty of money for food in the past but with all the guests we've had lately, the food budget is sort of strained, and I've had to use more hours for the maids. Part-time isn't enough to keep so many rooms open and the laundry done. Pierce and I don't complain, but we're both getting older, and could use more help with our duties. I love to cook but it gets demanding sometimes. Some help in the kitchen might be handy, although I'm not complaining."

"Miss Clio, you're not saying anything." He closed the ledger and turned to me.

"My life is perfectly comfortable because these two people see to it, and always have. Whatever changes would come about in our living arrangements and budgets should focus on them first; they carry the responsibilities of the household on their shoulders and have done so for years. Maybe I'd like some luxuries for myself, but I couldn't in good conscience ask for them until needs perceived by Mrs. Ryan and Pierce had been taken into consideration."

"Well," Evans said, "If you were to find me acceptable as executor and administrator, I think my first job would be to explore the resources that the estate can furnish for the household, untrammeled by the skimming that Horace Elder has undoubtedly perpetrated. I would guess they would be significantly more generous than they have been—just diverting the expense of maintaining Mr. Armand over to the basic operating budget for the household is bound to make a difference for you. How much of a difference I'm not prepared to say until I audit your books and Elder's accounts. However, if you are interested, I would be favorably disposed to an appointment as executor and administrator of Armand DeVille's will."

"I'd like to confer privately with Mrs. Ryan and Pierce; then I will give you an answer. Just wait a few minutes while the three of us adjourn to the library. Have another cup of coffee, why don't you? I'm sure the thermos is still hot."

The conference in the library was short and sweet. Pierce said it would be a pleasure to work with a *gentleman*, Mrs. Ryan gave him full credit for understanding the needs of the household on short notice, and I liked his judicious way of going about things. He had treated my two best friends courteously and kindly in complete recognition of their worth. That decided me. We returned to the dining room and I told Evans I would instruct Susan to notify Judge Abercrombie that I wanted him to appoint Carter Evans executor/administrator of the DeVille affairs. We shook hands all around, and then I took Mr. Evans on a tour of the house. Yellow crime scene tape still limited access to Papa's bedroom, the red bedroom where Elder had met his end, and Arnold Slocum's room. Smudges of fingerprinting dust disfigured the door jambs and had Mrs. Ryan itching to clean them up.

"What a handsome old place this is," Evans was saying as

we returned to the first floor and entered the library. “And what a wonderful place this room and books have been for Armand, and now you, to do your translating. May I see what you are currently working on?”

“Of course, although *The Metamorphoses* are my current project.”

“Fine, I’m also an adept of Latin and actually more up to date there than with Greek. I’ve been tempted to try translating the dramatists, Terence being my favorite. But I have been too busy to settle down to it.”

A little more small talk and Evans, who had asked me to call him Carter, said he had appointments to keep in the city. He left amid smiles from Mrs. Ryan and Pierce, and with one of those nice handshakes for me. As the sound of his car’s engine died away down the drive, the three of us looked at one another and flashed triumphant V-signs.

§ Thirty Three §

WINTER WAS LOSING its grip on the landscape. In the woods the snow was receding to disclose the green tips of crocuses and daffodils on the sunny slopes. I was feeling like the lone occupant of a small boat bobbing among rapids and eddies of a very active sea of changes and circumstances. Sheriff Land had pretty much wiped out Arnold Slocum's eddy. After extensive interrogation, Arnold had admitted to an addiction to Valium, Papa's prescribed medication. He had been stealing drugs regularly from the vials held ready at the bedside and making up the contents with water. When I had the chance, I asked Dr. Lev how it happened that the diluted drug had continued to control Papa's seizures, at least until that last failure. He said the concentration of the drug was so high that Arnold's judicious withdrawal and dilution had not affected effectiveness seriously until that last disastrous event. The sheriff had turned Arnold's case over to the district attorney who was planning to charge him with possession and use of controlled substances, namely the marijuana and the stolen vials of Valium found in his room. A further charge of contributing to the death of Armand DeVille was still possible but the DA was saving it for leverage to get Arnold to finger his marijuana supplier. The sheriff had dismissed me as a suspect in Papa's death, thank goodness.

I was still awhirl in Elder's orbit, however. Jud had been back on some errands for the sheriff and in his casual fashion had let slip that although the dagger bore no fingerprints, a wisp of white thread had been found between the edges of the wound and the hilt. That thread explained to me the search that had gone on in the house for gloves and had ended up at the box of a dozen or so pairs of white cotton gloves kept in the butler's pantry and used for handling polished silver and crystal. Jud said gleefully that the state forensics lab had made a perfect match of the thread in the wound with the material of the gloves in the pantry. Jud babbled on about absence of fingerprints on the dagger, and the presence of mine, Mrs. Ryan's, and Pierce's on other weapons in the trophy. Our prints were easily explained—four times a year we took the trophy apart and dusted and polished the arms that made it up. Mrs. Ryan would not allow the maids to touch it, lest they cut themselves on the knives and swords. One day, when Dr. Lev had dropped by with Mrs. Ryan's blood pressure prescription, I questioned him why there had been no significant amount of blood from Elder's wound. I had had a good look at the site of the wound and there was hardly a drop on Elder's pajama top. It seems that the blade of the dagger acted like a cork in the wound and Elder's position ensured that the bleeding from his punctured heart had drained into body cavities. When I asked how someone could get that close to Elder without his waking, Dr. Lev launched a sharp glance at me before he answered.

"There were traces of soluble barbiturate in the bedside carafe and a significant level in Elder's blood. I had not prescribed or furnished that drug and there was no sign of it among Elder's possessions. The current explanation is that drug had been added to the water in the carafe, and that Elder had drunk fairly deeply from it, and gone fast asleep while someone later dumped the contents of the carafe and refilled it with fresh water. The search of the house has so far failed to turn up any sign of barbiturates, even Arnold has been cleared of suspicion for them."

"Who brought the carafe in the beginning and who dumped it?" I inquired, dreading the answers.

Phrasing his answer carefully, Dr. Lev told me that Pierce admitted he had brought the carafe, filled with fresh water, so Elder could take Dr. Lev's prescription for gastric upset. That was around three P.M. Subsequently, Mrs. Bettle had been in and out every two hours, finding Elder deep in sleep and with perfectly normal pulse and respiration. At her final check at midnight, she poured out the contents of the carafe and refilled it from the bathroom tap.

So Elder was doped and whoever had doped him could have gone in and stabbed him after procuring gloves from the pantry and the dagger from the hall. It seemed that the solution to the murder might be discovery of a person in the house, who knew about the gloves and the dagger, had an unacknowledged supply of barbiturate, and could prowl silently around the sleeping household. Until a source of the drug could be pinned down, suspicion could well include me, Mrs. Ryan, and Pierce, and even Mrs. Bettle, as good possibilities, Tom and Susan as less probable suspects. And I was the only one with explicit motive! I shuddered and paled every time I thought about it, then made up my mind not to think about it.

The whirl at Elder-Thackeray created another set of eddies. They involved frequent visits of Carter and Susan, together or separately to Hauteville House, for conferences with me and Bonny Harvill; and Carter and Susan's pushing and pulling Tom and the auditors and agents at the offices of Elder-Thackeray for the DeVille documents. Carter and Susan were so often at the House, that they were leaving a changes of clothes and toiletries in the red and peacock bedrooms, respectively. Mrs. Ryan and Carter were working out expense budgets far more generous than Elder had allowed. Carter proposed a monthly allowance from which Mrs. Ryan would pay utility bills, staff salaries, food and supplies purchases, and minor maintenance costs from a checking account subject to my monthly countersigned review. I would write the checks for single expenditures which exceeded $2000. I would submit Mrs. Ryan's and my checkbooks quarterly to audit by Bonny Harvill, who would in turn report his findings to Carter. This arrangement would lapse when the complications of Elder's mismanagement had been resolved and the whole inheritance was turned over to me.

Funds in the fake Clio Felicia DeVille's account in the Bank of Erie had been retrieved and the balance transferred to an account in the real Clio Felicia Deville's (my) name in the Peoples Bank of Fairview. Ms. Marcia Pate was being prosecuted by the Bank of Erie for conspiracy to defraud, and although she was very likely to be convicted, the probability was slim that what she had spent of the money Elder had funneled to her would be recovered. Susan's investigator had uncovered two joint accounts in the names of fake-Felicia and Elder in country banks in Perry County, but dealing with them was more difficult because they were part of Elder's estate. But Susan was working on it! I called her Bulldog to tease her.

Carter had now arranged for the $600 monthly income specified by the trust to be paid into my personal account in the Peoples Bank. I had some doubts as to where and how I could spend that much money; at $20 a pop for a haircut every four weeks, a dollar here and a dollar there for cosmetics and sundries, $35 now and again for a new pair of jeans or a shirt, I wasn't sure I would use it up. When I told Carter my misgivings, he nearly fell out of his chair laughing.

"You're the first woman I ever encountered who didn't know how to spend money. I may have to hire a tutor to teach you." Then growing serious, he went on, "If you find you can't spend it, transfer it over to a savings account, let it accumulate, and then blow a big chunk on something special—a trip to Europe, a convertible, a fur coat."

My face was hot and red with embarrassment but he had reminded me that I wanted to do something for Mrs. Bettle. Papa's will had not recognized the years she had so faithfully nursed him (Carter said it was because the will was written before she was hired and never updated), but I thought she deserved at least an annuity, maybe $25,000. Might that be a place for the money I couldn't spend on myself. For a moment, I thought Carter was going to laugh again but instead, he just smiled, and said,

"All we have to do is buy her an annuity from the general fund of the estate. You don't have to give up your long-delayed allowance dollars. I can see to Mrs. Bettle's annuity right away. $25,000 you think? OK. Do you want to tell her or shall I do it with a formal letter?"

"Both. But let me tell her first so a formal letter won't surprise her into a heart attack, and then you send the letter so she has something concrete to treasure."

When I inquired as to the progress of investigations at Elder-Thackeray, Carter was very serious.

"Clio, the DeVille investments, with the exception of the bloc set aside from your mother and the trust, are in a mess. I should reassure you before I go further; at the moment, your income is coming from the trust; household expense is being paid out of the income from the reliable investments; neither of those sources of funds is at risk. The stocks and bonds Elder was managing—*mis*managing I should say—need the attention of an experienced financial consultant. For the time being, the A-G's auditor is plowing through them looking for evidence of fraud or theft. But as soon as he's finished I'm suggesting you let me engage a qualified financial consultant to study and restructure them. It's possible that Elder was merely careless or ill-advised in his buying and selling of assets; if so, cleaning up the portfolios will be relatively simple. If not, be prepared to see his estate and the partners of his misdeeds spending a long time in court. There is already enough evidence in the cases of other clients to bring charges against the two co-conspirators. In the meantime, I want to reassure you again—the bulk of your father's assets still exist and although their value may have been diminished, they are still substantial. "

"I'm almost glad I didn't know until now how he betrayed Papa's trust." I said. "I would have really had a motive for revenge by drastic means."

Carter chuckled, "Don't let Curtis Land hear you say anything like that. He still has you at the top of his list of suspects for Elder's murder."

"I'm sure that's true, but why hasn't he done anything about it? I keep waiting for the other shoe to drop. Nothing. He doesn't even come by to ask questions."

"I think his evidence is too weak to convince the DA there's a case. Motive, means, and opportunity do not *always* add up to a smoking gun. Just hang in there. Now, to change the subject, would you like to go with me to the Monet exhibition in Erie next Saturday? This is the last week and everyone is raving about it. We could drive up in the morning, do the exhibit, have a nice dinner and drive back all in one day."

"A date? Are you asking me on a date?" I mumbled, then I got my answer out clear and positive, "I'd love to, what time do we leave?"

Carter said he would come down on Friday night and we would leave after a late breakfast. I was thrilled. I hadn't been to a museum or art exhibit since I was 12 and the current governess thought I should see the Da Vinci sketches. I spent the rest of the week in happy anticipation and shopping for a classy outfit.

§ Thirty Four §

In view of past demands on my life, I had never seen much point in spending much time in front of a mirror. Making sure my face was clean, teeth brushed, and hair combed seemed adequate grooming. But when primping for my date with Carter, a close look at my appearance almost shocked me. I realized that frequent outdoor exercise had wiped away worry wrinkles and dark circles under my eyes and had restored youthful bloom to my skin. Thanks to regular visits to Sally's salon, my hair had grown thicker and more lustrous, and because of her advice, routine use of an understated rose-red lipstick had emphasized the whiteness of my teeth. "Clio," I said to myself, "can it be that I'm pretty?" I needed no more answer than the major boost to my self-confidence I felt.

Consequently, the date on Saturday was, for me, a stunning success. Garbed in a black faille pants suit with a scarlet shell, wearing a diamond pin I found in Felicia's jewel box, shod in sensible black patent leather shoes, I felt like a fashion plate. Mrs. Duncan had insisted I needed a top coat and hauled out a selection that ranged from fake fur to real mink. I finally chose a silk shawl she had draped for display on a mannequin (scarlet roses on a black background, fringes) and she grudgingly agreed it was a nice touch, but cautioned that it wouldn't be warm enough if the weather turned. She gave in graciously enough in the end. I knew my outfit was a success when I saw the admiration on Carter's face; Mrs. Ryan and Pierce had passed enthusiastic approval on it when I tried it on for their inspection on Friday.

Carter and I chatted comfortably on the trip to Erie. Spring, albeit a bit chilly, was in command of the weather and the roadsides were green and blooming with wildflowers. Carter was an expert driver and his Mercedes seemed to ride on air. When I later reviewed the topics of our conversation, I wondered if I had not done most of the talking. Tales of my childhood, struggles and surprises with tutors and governesses, Mrs. Ryan and Pierce always there with hot chocolate and cookies, Papa a remote presence in the library, only occasionally appearing at the dinner table. Carter told me he had noticed and liked the blue elephant in the morning room, and pride and modesty struggled together in my reply. We arrived at the museum at opening time, wandered happily through authentic art in the exhibit rooms for two hours, lunched in the museum restaurant (the décor was marvelous, food mediocre), and went to the Cinema Center for a movie (*avant garde*, a Cannes prize winner for photography, entitled *BOO* for no apparent reason, I don't think it was intended as a comedy but we nevertheless laughed or snickered throughout, the plot and dialog were so ludicrous.) We made it to the posh dining room in the penthouse of Carter's club just in time to be greeted with great ceremony by a tuxedoed *maitre d'* who seated us with a magnificent view of the lake. Sunset and our meal occurred at the same time, I could barely eat for looking at the scene—both outside and inside the room. Elegantly gowned ladies, smartly suited gentlemen, many of them Carter's acquaintances. I gawked unashamedly like the naïve country girl I was. When I finally settled down to eating, I found the food excellent but not much better than Mrs. Ryan's on one of her *fête* days. I was grateful for my previous exposure to canapés, lobster, veal marsala, truffles, *petit pois*, and Sacher torte. My gustatory education had been as thorough as my training in table manners. By the time we finished our meal, a jeweled necklace of lights studded the dark along the waterfront, their distorted, shimmering reflections in the water every bit as gorgeous as their origins on land. I leaned back from my coffee and sighed happily. Everything was so wonderful;

the realization of my ignorance of the world outside of Hauteville House and Fairview was slowly dawning on me. I realized that it was dawning on Carter also. On the way home, I felt obliged to explain how it had come about. First, it was from keeping Papa's hours for my classical education and translations, then it was from spending eight hours a day at his bedside, never a day or weekend off. And, then too, from being alone, except for the nurses and servants, with limited forms of entertainment such as walks in the woods, visits to dentists and drugstores, Mrs. Ryan's gourmet meals just to break the monotony of our lives. Carter simply listened and nodded, asking an occasional question. When I ran down, he asked the ultimate question,

"Why didn't you ever rebel? I know you were reared to civility and good manners but you don't strike me as being mentally incompetent or pathologically timid. Weren't you ever angry or resentful? The nannies, tutors, and governesses, and Mrs. Ryan and Pierce saw to your basic needs—as they defined them. But the basic needs of being a social being in a world outside Hauteville House—why were those never perceived nor met? I'm surprised your psyche wasn't warped."

"Maybe it is!" I said mournfully. "In the last year I found I had so much hate harbored in my heart and mind—hate for the house, for Papa, for my life. Now I'm ashamed of such feelings, and I haven't really put them behind me. I may always have them, or at least will always remember them. But some good things have happened, too. I've seesawed between hate and happiness for the past year until I hardly know what I feel. I wonder sometimes if my bottled up hate was vented as resentment of Horace Elder. But," I hastened to add, "I never hated him enough to murder him "

Carter chuckled and reached over to pat my knee in a comradely fashion.

"Well, I hope you are going to give me a chance to introduce you to the world outside of Hauteville House. I hope you enjoy my company because I certainly enjoy yours. I'd like to plan more excursions to introduce you to a world of fun and excitement. Are you game?"

"Oh, yes," I breathed. Now, I knew how Clement Moore's kids felt, with visions of sugarplums dancing in their heads. It was nearly midnight as we got back to the House and we parted on the second floor landing, exchanging thanks and handshakes as we went off to our rooms. I thought I would be too excited to sleep but I did, and dreamed of sugarplums.

§ Thirty Five §

Spring was glorious. Cool nights, warm days, woods full of wildflowers, spring cleaning in the House, spring in my steps, just plain spring all over. Much to my delight Carter seemed to be making me a project. Every weekend was an event, dinner and a play (touring company of *Cats*) in Erie, maple syrup festival at a farm over in Perry County (a chance to OD on pancakes and sausage), a huge fleamarket in Deerfield (Carter was looking for antique hardware for a bureau he was refinishing), a "house walk" in Fairview (who would have thought such a small town had six historic homes fully restored). My translations went definitely on the back burner. I found them boring! I was spending my time shopping for new clothes, walking in the woods, directing the two lads Mrs. Ryan had hired to clean up the parterres. The vista between the house and the far edge of the woods was being mowed regularly and consequently becoming a treat to view from the morning room and dining room windows. The boys were hard workers but had trouble telling a perennial from a weed and my intervention saved many a specimen plant from the compost heap. When I looked in the mirror, I saw my complexion growing tan, my worry wrinkles vanishing and my eyes glowing. Mrs. Ryan was in fine fettle; she had enough money to hire window washing, carpet beating, and floor and furniture waxing. A house clean and sparkling to her satisfaction was a foretaste of heaven. Pierce had the Cadillac out of the garage and spent hours washing and polishing the exterior and vacuuming the interior. Mrs. Ryan allowed him to purchase new tires and order a tune up at the shop in the village. He begged for opportunities to drive me to Fairview on my personal errands, I suspected so he could park his darling car at the curb and take bows for its splendid condition.

Carter called on the 22nd of May to tell me he had a meeting set up for us at Elder-Thackeray on the 25th. Could I meet him there at 9 A.M.?

"Of course," I said, "but where is it?"

I was instructed to check my e-mail for a marked map. I did but when I showed it to Pierce, he said he didn't need it, had often driven Papa there in the old days. As we drove to the appointment I pumped Pierce for advice on purchasing a car for myself and learning to drive. If I could drive myself, my pitch went, I wouldn't have to trouble him to drive me around. But he bridled and answered, with a trace of asperity,

"Miss Clio, it's no trouble. It's grand to spend time on the road again with this car. It's been too little used for so long, rarely out of the garage more than once a week, and then only in good weather. With the new tires, it rides smooth as silk, doesn't it? Aren't you happy with my driving? I passed my last tests at the license bureau perfectly and...."

"That's not it, Pierce," I interrupted. "It's that I want to learn how to drive. How many women my age have never driven a car? I think if I could drive, I'd feel that I had finally grown up. Would you teach me? What kind of car should I get? Would you look after it like you do this one?"

I got a grudging promise out of him for a day to visit Fairview VW together to look at runabouts. I confessed I had fallen in love with Bonny's bug and wanted one myself. Pierce tried to dampen my enthusiasm by bringing up every criticism of VWs that he had ever read; he shook his head gloomily as he predicted I would be disappointed in my choice. However, his spirits picked up after I convinced him he was in a position to play a serious role in my automotive future: invaluable for advice in making my selection, essential to my driving lessons, and necessary for maintenance of the new vehicle

As we talked a bit of pollen flew in the open window and into my eye. I opened the glove compartment to get a Kleenex. I had to rummage for the purse-size packet and in the process, unearthed a prescription vial full of red capsules. I gave the label only a quick glance, saw Pierce's name, and pushed the vial back under the other stuff. Then I successfully extracted the mote in my eye and we traveled on companionably, pulling up in front of Elder-Thackeray behind Carter's Mercedes at exactly 8:55. Pierce leaped out, whipped around the car, and ushered me out with as much panache as if I were a queen. I was coming to the sad realization that my and Papa's way of life had drained joy out of Pierce's life. Trained from boyhood for ceremony and high style, he had had little opportunity to exercise either once Papa became a recluse and made me one as well. Rejuvenation and happiness for him lay in performing again familiar everyday duties in familiar everyday ways now that Hauteville House and its inhabitants had wakened from a 15-year sleep.

Carter was coming down the steps to see me into the building which was a handsome modern version of a Georgian mansion. He led me past an elegant reception area now cluttered with desks and computer workstations and down a hall to a sumptuous board room with a deep bay filled with a jungle of live tropical plants, blooming with colorful orchids and bromeliads. Here Bonny, Susan, and Thomas greeted me warmly and Thomas introduced me to two middle-aged, poker-faced men in superbly tailored suits. One of them was Deputy Attorney General Warner, the other Mr. Bennett, an IRS auditor. A mousy young man was seated unobtrusively at a stenotype, fingers poised, and his tape recorder at the ready. As everyone settled into chairs, Mr. Warner voiced a list of the persons in attendance, and then took charge of the meeting.

"We're here to evaluate Ms. DeVille's claim to documents pertaining to the DeVille estate. The state's review and the federal review, although not complete, have progressed far enough that we can consider releasing copies to Ms. DeVille's legal representatives. The originals must remain in the corpus of Elder-Thackeray records until all state and federal investigations of Horace Elder's activities have been completed. However, before we release the material, we wish to have on record Ms. DeVille's *viva voce* justification for acquiring the documents. May we hear from you, Ms. DeVille?"

I was somewhat taken aback. I expected to depend on Susan and Carter to speak on my behalf, but if I had to, I would do my best. I started with a brief summary of Papa's disability as his reason for giving Horace Elder power of attorney, indicated roughly the period in which Elder had been in total financial control of DeVille affairs, and confessed to total ignorance of the arrangements until just a few months ago. I suggested Mr. Harvill be asked to review his examination of the documents we found stored at Hauteville House and how we came to suspect Elder's handling of DeVille affairs. Mr. Warner then invited Bonny to contribute his information. Bonny hauled a neatly printed report out of his briefcase and handed it to Warner, then proceeded verbally to summarize his findings prior to Elder's death and subsequently when Carter engaged him to continue working with the documents at the House. The bottom line consisted of two major findings. The first was the bank account in my name, fed from my mother's legacy in trust, but hidden from the time of my sixteenth birthday when payouts to tutors and governesses had lapsed, and recently tapped for the benefit of Marcia Pate. The second was the unexplained disappearance of securities shown in portfolio listings until five or six years ago, but missing from Elder's subsequent annual reports to Papa.

As Bonny concluded his speech, Mr. Bennett took the floor to say that all income to the DeVille accounts and holdings had been faithfully reported and all taxes had been paid. The IRS would have no claim on the DeVille estate; in fact, the IRS was ready to release the tax documents from Elder's office to any investigation of diversion of funds or resources. He noted that they would substantiate the original existence and subsequent sale of certain securities. He made the point that although Elder's records showed sale of those securities, they gave no indication of disposition of the money realized by the sale. The IRS was still looking for assets Elder had hidden away for himself without paying taxes on them. The DeVille estate was free from claims but claims were likely against Elder's estate—providing, of course, the hidden funds were located. Bad news for his widow!

Then it was Susan's turn to describe her efforts to reclaim assets that belonged to the DeVille estate. So far only the bank account in the name of the fake Clio had been recovered. Susan's private investigator had unearthed two accounts set up in joint ownership with my and Elder's names in Deerfield and Erie banks. Whether these accounts held the money realized from the securities that had vanished from the portfolio Elder managed, there was no telling. Nothing could be done until Elder's estate was proved, or hard evidence of the origin of the contents of these accounts was acquired. A claim might later be made against the Elder estate for money fraudulently obtained but for now, Susan recommended waiting and watching.

Carter's contribution was to present the scheme of reorganization of the DeVille estate; his report corroborated securities gone missing without explanation and specified their market values as of the last time they were known to exist. He was not optimistic that those assets or proceeds from their sale would be recovered, although Susan's investigations might yet bear fruit. Otherwise, he was confident that the trust held by the First National Bank of Columbus was in good shape and that the stocks and bonds remaining in Elder's office portfolio were properly accounted for. He was recommending to the probate judge that the terms of Armand's will be executed as the estate currently stood. He mentioned briefly that he was recommending to me the engagement of a certified financial advisor to manage the portfolio with my participation and input.

Mr. Warner was rather glassy-eyed by the time all of this

information had been put on the table but he rallied to ask Tom whether he had anything to add.

"No, sir." Tom said, "Only that I have had Xerox copies made of all the DeVille documents found in the Elder-Thackeray files and am prepared to turn over these notarized copies to Ms. DeVille's lawyer. Although the originals remain the property of the Elder estate, Mrs. Elder has agreed to give access to them to both the Attorney General's office and to Ms. DeVille's legal counsel should a justified need arise. In order to hand over the documents, I require Ms. DeVille's signature on numerous lists. The stock certificates and bonds held in this office will be placed in Mr. Carter Evans's hands, after he has appended his signature to the inventory list in his capacity as executor and administrator of the estate."

With that, Tom placed two document storage boxes and a metal lockbox on the table. Mr. Warner heaved a sigh of relief and said,

"So far as I can see, this meeting has achieved its purpose and as soon as the signings have been completed, I declare it adjourned. Does anyone disagree? No? Very well, start signing."

§ Thirty Six §

Having survived almost terminal writer's cramp, I joined Carter, Susan, and Bonny for a late lunch at a nearby hotel. Tom pled further meetings with Warner and Bennett and bade us goodbye but I caught a whispered exchange between him and Susan that scheduled dinner at seven. My hunch was right, the two of them had something going and my blessing went with them. As we went our respective ways, Carter made a date to come to Hauteville House on Friday so we could go together to the Peoples Bank and Trust of Fairview and place the contents of the metal lockbox into a safety deposit box, for which I would hold the key. I was also given the key to another safety deposit box that held Felicia's jewelry (the first I had heard of that!). More evidence that I was grown up and responsible for my own affairs! Susan had taken custody of the DeVille papers for reviewing, sorting, looking for evidence in case of legal action against Elder's estate. The more I thought about it, however, the more reluctant I found myself to drag out and pursue settlement of these issues. Maybe we could just write off the losses; I'd think more about that after I had achieved a better grasp of the value of the estate. But my immediate reaction was charitable. Why prosecute a man for his misdeeds beyond the grave? Why harass the widow innocent of his misdeeds?

I was tired and on the trip back to the House dozed in the back seat under the car robe Pierce threw over me. I dreamed and in my dream kept seeing a vial of bright red capsules moving from one anonymous hand to another. I woke at the House, the memory of my dream fading quickly into that limbo where dreams go when real life supervenes. Mrs. Ryan greeted me with a message from Mallory the undertaker. He was ready to inter Papa's ashes in the family cemetery whenever I found it convenient. Mrs. Ryan asked whether to plan for a gathering of friends but I opted to ask only the Reverend McLinn for a few words as she, Pierce, and I stood by. We made arrangements for the following Wednesday. Mrs. Bettle asked to join the party; she was leaving on Friday for her son's house in Florida and to start a life away from Hauteville House. She obviously thought that seeing her long-time patient into the ground was an appropriate valedictory to the House and the DeVilles. I had never felt the same degree of intimacy and attachment for her that I had for Mrs. Ryan and Pierce but I nevertheless felt kindly toward her and blessed her for the faithful care she had given Papa for so long. Of course, she was invited to the interment. Then, as it happened, Carter arrived without notice that morning with some papers for me to sign and it seemed natural to invite him to join us. I didn't expect the event to be emotional for us, although Mrs. Bettle's tears were a given. And so it transpired. I had supervised the boys weeding and mowing the long-neglected grounds of the cemetery inside its wrought iron fence. The weather was beautiful and rustling leaves of the century-old oaks provided music. Next to Felicia's headstone at the foot of the monumental marble angel, another simple headstone had been set to mark Papa's place. A sheaf of red carnations covered what I knew was a small neat hole to receive the urn. Reverend McLinn read psalms and favorite gospel passages, and it was done. Mallory's man was closing the grave as we walked cheerfully back to the House. Another chapter closed, another layer of hate fading away.

On Friday, we gave Mrs. Bettle a festive sendoff. I had found a handsome gold necklace at the jewelry store in the village and had a pendant engraved with her initials and inclusive dates of her stay at Hauteville House. Tears, as usual, expressed her emotions at parting and bathed the memento as I put it around her neck.

Pierce and I drove her to the Erie airport and saw her off from the gate, waving and promising to write often. I was impressed by Pierce's sophisticated navigation of the lanes and parking lots around the airport. He said Papa had traveled frequently by air when I was a child and Pierce had chauffeured him to and from the terminal. No one had ever thought to take me to see an airport, so I made him show me around before we went home. I chalked the tour up as another mark on my list of grownup experiences. I seemed to be accumulating a lot of them these days.

§ Thirty Seven §

SPRING FLOWED PEACEFULLY into summer and my happiness bloomed with the flowers. I was happier than I had been since carefree childhood. The gloom that once haunted Hauteville House seemed to dissolve in the sunlight and cool breezes coming in at the freshly washed windows. Mrs. Ryan bustled about, supervising long-desired and long-delayed repairs and refurbishing. The shabby furniture in the morning room was decked out in fresh chintz covers. Glaziers had mended dozens of panes in the conservatory and we had made a start to restore plantings and get the fountain working again. The Oriental rugs were sent out for a wash and returned in all their bright original colors. Pierce had taken me to the Vickers VW dealership and helped me pick out a runabout. He spent an hour contentedly inspecting the inside of the engine compartment, passing judgment on the quality of the workmanship, and finally approving a purchase. He withheld approval of the lipstick red model I chose; to his mind red was no color for a car but if that's what I wanted.... Then the driving lessons started. He was a patient and thorough teacher, and as soon as I could negotiate the roads on the estate without incident, he took me to the BMV in the village to get a learner's permit. We practiced every day for one or two hours on the country roads around the estate and after two weeks he decided I was ready to test for my license. That went off well and soon I was running my scarlet bug back and forth to the village on every frivolous errand Mrs. Ryan or I could think of.

By an enormous effort of will, I sat down again to the

translations of *The Metamorphoses*, disciplining myself to spend at least 4 hours at it every day. My sheaf of manuscript had grown to 50 double-spaced pages when Marcus Atwater gave me a call. Would I be willing to send what I had to date so that he might shop it around among some possibly interested parties, he asked. I said sure, expect something in tomorrow's mail. Carter came down the next day to take me on what he called "a summer jaunt." As we were leaving for a destination unknown (to me), I told him about sending my manuscript to Atwater. He did not approve; when asked why, he said I needed to copyright my stuff before it left my hands and fell into the hands of literary pirates. I burst into laughter at the a ridiculous notion that my unpretentious little translations might be stolen to profit an unscrupulous editor somewhere. He proceeded to give me a lecture.

"Those translations have more value than little books to be sold to and read by a handful of esthetes and dilettantes enamored of classic literature. Think of them as grist for movies, made-for-television or big screen productions. Think of them as intellectual property with a potential for making big money in the right—or wrong—hands. There's quite a market for scripts and scenarios that can be worked up with heavily-muscled bare-chested male stars and big-bosomed, barely-clothed females. Why should your property be put at risk by Marcus Atwater's naiveté? He's a nice guy with nice guy acquaintances in a rather esoteric publishing environment but an innocent after all, easy prey for hungry pirates."

I was unconvinced, "So what? I don't need to make money off of the translations. You tell me I've got plenty in the bank, enough to last me for the rest of my life and then some."

"It's the principle of the thing, Clio. You have to learn to think things through. There's no sense in setting yourself up as a target for unprincipled predators to take advantage of. I don't think Marcus Atwater has dark designs, nor will putting your translations in his hands probably do any harm, now or later. I just want to caution you to THINK before you jump into some project feet first. Now, lecture's over. Get in the car please and let's be off."

Our destination turned out to be a magnificent, enormous amusement park on the lakeshore. No governess I had ever had would have approved of eating cotton candy, playing DodgeEm, prowling the Fun House, eating corn dogs on a stick, trying to shoot tin ducks moving across the back of a gallery. Even less would she have approved the water slide and the roller coaster, although the merry-go-round might have been acceptable. I had a wonderful time eating every indigestible viand my greed led me to. Carter accompanied me in every venture with an indulgent smile and no obvious signs of apprehension. He whooped as loudly as I on the killer decline of the roller coaster but admitted that unlike me, he had no appetite for ice cream afterwards. We seemed to have done it all; when after a hasty wash up, I climbed in the passenger seat for the trip home and promptly fell asleep.

When Carter had pulled up in front of the House, he reached over to jiggle my shoulder and asked, "Did you have a good time?"

"Um hmm," I answered, only half awake. "How about you?"

"Best time I've ever had since my dad took me there when I was ten. That was forty five years ago. I relived all the wonder today, the more so because I saw the wonder in your eyes. And I loved reliving it in your company. Yes, I had a good time."

"Are you coming in?" I inquired. "I better warn you. I intend to ask Mrs. Ryan for chicken broth and crackers, maybe some milk, for supper. But she would rustle up something more substantial for you, I'm sure."

He chuckled and declined the invitation. He had appointments in town in the morning and he was tuckered out from his big day. He would see me later in the week to go over selected stock holdings. I bade him good-bye and went in. Mrs. Ryan and Pierce listened with amusement as I enthusiastically recapitulated the details of my day. I got my supper of broth and crackers and went off to bed, still remembering with delight the swoosh of the long drop of the roller coaster. I remembered something else and did some calculations. If Carter had gone to the park when he was ten, and that was forty five years ago, he must be 55, only 18 years older than I. I went to sleep with that agreeable bit of information tucked away in the back of my mind.

§ Thirty Eight §

I went down to breakfast the next morning still basking the euphoria of my wonderful fun day. As I sat down, Pierce reminded me that Vickers at the VW agency was expecting to make a mandated adjustment to the seat belt mechanism of my car today.

"I polished and vacuumed it yesterday. I could take it in for you if you'd like," he offered, clearly expecting me to turn down his offer. He knew I lost no opportunity to drive my scarlet bug, no matter how trivial the trip.

"There's a short list of things to pick up for me, if you have time." Mrs. Ryan said.

Of course, I took the list and set off happily about nine A.M. Mr. Vickers told me the repair would take about an hour if I was willing to wait and showed me into the waiting room. The TV was on and I was watching the TODAY crew go through their morning routine, when Sheriff Land came through from the service area.

"Hello there, Ms. DeVille. I saw your little red car in there and parked my official car right next to it. Are you enjoying your new wheels?"

"I certainly am. I'm glad to run into you; I've been intending to drop into your office and ask how your investigation of Mr. Elder's death is going. I hope you are making progress."

Land gave me a quizzical look before he drawled,

"Well, yes and no. We need just a couple more bits of evidence before we can say yes, but they seem to be hard to come by. May I ask if anyone besides yourself drives your little car?"

"Not so far, although Pierce often puts it in or gets it out of the garage. He doesn't really approve of it—the color, you know; but he is faithful in caring for it. Why do you ask?"

"Just curious. Owners of new red cars are usually pretty protective of them, wouldn't you say? Don't much care for anyone else to drive them."

I laughed, "You are so right, but don't you think I'm entitled? I've waited for a lot of years to have and drive a car of my own."

"Yes, of course. Nice seeing you." And he tipped his hat and left.

Not long after, the service manager came in to say the car was ready. So I did Mrs. Ryan's errands and got back home by lunch time. A few days later, Sheriff Land called, asking me to come by his office. Said he had a few questions, wouldn't take long, tomorrow morning perhaps? Naturally, I agreed and presented myself at the reception desk at the County Justice Center at 8 A.M., mildly curious as to what questions still remained to be asked. At the time of the murder, every one of us in the House had answered questions until we were hoarse. Something must have turned up. When the deputy on duty at the desk showed me into Land's office, he rose to greet me and offer me a chair. I expected law officers to have messy desks, or at least desks with in/out boxes, blotters, and pen/pencil sets, but the surface of the Sheriff's desk was absolutely bare. After a bit of friendly chit chat, Land reached into a desk drawer and removed a file folder and placed it in the exact center of that bare surface. When opened, the folder disclosed several sheets of computer printout and a small plastic bag with a red bead in it. Land then began the conversation that would blow my mind.

Holding up the printouts, he said, "These are reports from the state forensic lab, detailing analysis of the traces of drug found in Elder's carafe, and the levels in his blood at the time of death, and the contents of this capsule. The capsule came from your car. I saw it fall to the floor as the technician was shaking out the carpet. I recognized the capsule at once as bearing on our investigation of Horace Elder's murder and I picked it up in my handkerchief and packaged it in an evidence bag for analysis and to be tested for fingerprints. Incidentally, picking it up from the floor precludes your lawyer claiming illegal search and seizure. However, I must inform you that the analyses of drug from the carafe, from Elder's blood, and from this capsule," he waved the plastic bag at me, "confirm identity. The drug from each source is a perfect match."

I knew that I had gone pale, my breath was coming in gasps, my heart was pounding. The smoking gun! A source for the drug that stupefied Elder so that the murderer's blow could be struck in his sleep! In my car! How could it be? The missing link that had baffled the investigation. But I had never had anything like that red capsule, couldn't imagine how it had got in my car, the car had not come into my possession until six weeks ago, and there had been no other rider in it since. Pierce drove himself or Mrs. Ryan on their personal errands in the Cadillac. I was speechless.

Land continued, "The drug is a barbiturate called Seconal, often prescribed for sleeplessness...."

I interrupted, "One capsule, there must be more somewhere. Why didn't your searches of the house find it? Didn't you ask everyone if they took sleeping pills? I certainly don't and never have. Are you accusing me of having such pills? Even if I did, what would I be doing with them in my car?"

Land listened, patience written all over his face, then said, "I'm advising you to have your lawyer present before our conversation goes any further. I'm willing to continue it tomorrow after you have contacted Ms. LeMoine. I am assuming she is still your lawyer. Shall we meet again at 1 P.M. tomorrow?"

I nodded, too numb to say anything more. If he wanted me to have a lawyer at my elbow for questions tomorrow, this was a serious development. I walked out of the Justice Center with my head in a whirl and sat in my car for a good ten minutes before I felt ready to drive away. While I sat there my gaze wandered around the dash and the glove compartment door. Suddenly I suspected the car had been searched—without my permission—while I was in Land's office. But what could I do about that now except call Susan and confide my suspicions to her.

"Did you see anybody poking around in your car?" she asked after I had told her of my experiences that morning. No, I said, it was just a feeling.

"Well, don't let anybody touch the car until I get there. I'll be along early tomorrow morning. Keep your cool. They haven't anything on you yet, despite one red capsule. Try not to worry. I'll see you soon."

I didn't promise not to worry. How could I not worry? But I did go out to tell Pierce that I would put the car in the garage and to tell him not to get in it, polish it, or wash it. When he asked why, I said that Susan wanted to look it over in the morning before the Sheriff did tomorrow afternoon. When he asked why anybody wanted to look it over, I broke down and told him through my tears and sobs about the capsule. His face grew very serious and he came over to me, put his arm around my shoulders, and led me in to be comforted by Mrs. Ryan. We made a very gloomy threesome around the supper table and I went up to bed at seven o'clock, wishing I *did* have sleeping pills. I could have used one to quell the thoughts running through my head. But I finally did fall into a wakeful sleep. In one of my waking spells, I decided to let Carter know in the morning what was going on.

§ Thirty Nine §

Gloom persisted over breakfast and, for me, grew when I phoned Carter. Out of town, Washington DC, not back until end of the week, his secretary told me. Susan arrived around nine o'clock, garbed in a pants suit made of some silvery space age fabric, shod in her trademark patent leather boots. She glittered in the sunlight as she made me stand back to observe as she went over my car with the proverbial fine tooth comb. Nothing more to find, although I did detect a rearrangement of papers in the glove compartment and maps in the driver's door side pocket. That tended to confirm my suspicion of an unauthorized search yesterday. The mystery of the red capsule remained.

When Susan stepped back from her search, she was frowning. "Have you *ever* seen any sign or heard any word of sleeping pills in the House? How about red capsules? Mrs. Ryan? Pierce? Any of your guests? Carter maybe? I can assure you I'm clean."

Her query jogged my memory and I told her of the prescription vial I glimpsed as I rummaged in the glove compartment of the Cadillac; but that was weeks earlier, the day we all met at Elder-Thackeray to settle with the Attorney General and the IRS.

"Well," Susan said. "Where's the Caddy now? In the garage? Let's just give it a look."

I led the way to the garage. Since Arnold was gone, Pierce no longer locked the car and the glove compartment was entirely accessible, its contents neatly arranged and no sign of a prescription vial or red pills. Susan was about to search under carpets and seats when Pierce appeared, his face half-puzzled, half-miffed.

"May I be of help, Miss Clio? Miss Susan? What are you looking for? If it's dirt, I can assure you I cleaned the interior thoroughly yesterday, not that it needed it."

I reassured him that we did not distrust the efficiency of his car care. We were just checking in case anyone had left any medications in the glove box.

He responded firmly, stiffly respectful, "I would have found it if anything unusual was there, Miss Clio."

"Of course," I said and beckoned to Susan to leave for the house. Still no explanation for the red capsule.

"I want to talk to Mrs. Ryan," Susan said. "I'm going to ask to look at her blood pressure medication."

I persuaded Susan to let me do the asking, Mrs. Ryan might be insulted by such a question from an outsider. In the event, the medication consisted of two kinds of chalky-looking pills, yellow and white, a far cry from red capsules. Mrs. Ryan was only a little bit put out by the request, thank goodness, and prepared an early lunch for us without rancor.

When Susan and I were ushered into Sheriff Land's office, we found him in company with an assistant DA, his looks so youthful I wondered if he shaved yet. The lad was introduced as Milo Berger, and his subsequent questions made clear a sharp adult intelligence behind his baby face. He went over the salient points of the evidence in the Elder case, concluding with the red capsule, still in the plastic bag on display on the sheriff's desk. He refreshed his memory occasionally by reference to a bulky dossier also displayed on the desk. Susan kept silent, making voluminous notes on a yellow pad. My answers to Berger's questions were brief, absolutely truthful, but never straying from the point of the questions—just as Susan had counseled me as we drove in for the meeting. Although she had not explicitly instructed me to refrain from mentioning our private searches of the cars in the morning, I did refrain. I felt acutely uncomfortable with an evolving suspicion that Pierce had some connection with the red capsules.

After an hour and a half of Q&A, Berger concluded with, "I consider it my duty to report the results of my inquiry here to the District Attorney, with a recommendation to take them to the grand jury. I'm sure Ms. DeVille and her counsel realize that the grand jury may hand down an indictment of Ms. DeVille based on the weight of the current evidence."

Susan asked one question, "Were there fingerprints on the capsule?"

Berger reluctantly admitted none were found.

As Susan and I left the room, I maintained my outward composure although my heart was beating fast and my guts were quaking. A stop at the ladies' room was mandatory to rid myself of lunch. Susan waited outside, face impassive when I emerged. But she burst into speech as soon as we were safely in her car and had pulled away to go home.

"They haven't a thing on you. The grand jury threat is just that, a threat. The circumstantial evidence is so flimsy, the grand jurors will laugh it out of court."

"Susan, I can't take this calmly. I know I'm not guilty of Elder's murder. But you know, and I know, and neither of us are saying it—the circumstantial evidence we have points at *Pierce*—familiarity with white cotton gloves and with the dagger in the trophy, a vial of capsules that are probably Seconal once concealed in the car he considers his baby, access to the carafe, access to Elder's bedroom in the wee hours of the night. Dear God, what if it all adds up? That man has been more of a father to me than my own father."

And I burst into tears; fortunately Susan was driving. She pulled off on the verge of the country road, shut off the engine, and turned to me, holding out a wad of Kleenex.

"I've been waiting for this. Ever since you put two and two together from the vial of red capsules in the glove box and the red capsule the Sheriff says came from your car, you've been considering, consciously or subconsciously, Pierce as the owner of those red capsules. The Caddy his personal pride, your bug his new baby to clean inside and out—it adds up. The only minus to consider is the absence of fingerprints on that capsule. Nevertheless you can't ignore the total."

"But what can I do?" I moaned.

"Two choices: go quietly to the grand jury, keep mum about red capsules in the glove box, take your chances with the jury; or tell Pierce what you suspect, report your suspicions to the Sheriff, and watch the focus of the investigation shift. Neither choice is palatable but there they are. Choose."

I hunkered down, one solid blob of misery in the passenger seat of Susan's car, then I gathered my resolve and made a third choice. I opted to put off my decision until tomorrow.

"Let's go home, I'll do something tomorrow." I said.

Susan set the car in motion again. I invited her to stay the night. Whatever I decided tomorrow, I would need her to back me up.

§ Forty §

SUSAN DISAPPEARED INTO the peacock room and (I learned later) worked her cell phone, dispatching her private investigator on an emergency canvass of pharmacies within a 50-mile radius of Hauteville House. Her orders were to find out if any of them had dispensed to a George Alan Pierce in the past year. I asked Mrs. Ryan for an early dinner, and explained my red and swollen eyes with the truth—I was under threat of a grand jury to indict me for murder. Saying it aloud didn't make it any easier to accept but spilling to a sympathetic and incredulous ear was cathartic. We ate our dinners in a dreary silence although Susan excused herself three times to go to the morning room and confer with her cell phone. By now Mrs. Ryan's eyes were red and swollen too, and she was decorously dabbing her handkerchief to her eyes at intervals. Pierce, who had certainly been put in the picture by Mrs. Ryan, seemed unmoved; he sat without looking up from his plate, stolidly eating his sweet potatoes and pork chop and reaching for a second biscuit.

We all went to bed early, tired out by the ebb and swell of the day's emotions. I again slept poorly, waking often, rising for a drink of water twice, each time spending a few minutes looking out the window at the vista lit by moonlight and traversed by a troop of cavorting rabbits. At dawn, I finally slept, heavily and dreamlessly. The room was bright with morning sunlight when Susan's repeated knocks on my door woke me. Throwing on my robe, I got up and let her in.

"John, my PI, found a drugstore in Deerfield last night where a

George Alan handed in a prescription for Seconal in January, and twice since. John had to spend some dollars to get the information but I think it was worth it."

I nodded unhappily. Just then Mrs. Ryan came down the hall.

"It's Pierce," she said. "He hasn't come down for breakfast and he's always down by 6. I knocked on his door but he didn't answer. I'm worried. He hasn't been himself lately."

I led a procession to Pierce's door and knocked repeatedly, then tried the doorknob. It wasn't locked so I pushed the door open. Pierce was lying on his bed, wearing his dress shirt and coat, as if ready for receiving the guests arriving for a formal party. His face was calm and serene, his chest motionless. I hurried to him and picked up his wrist. It was stiff and cold, no pulse. I turned to Susan and Mrs. Ryan, still in the doorway.

"I think he's dead," I said, incredulous. "How could that happen?"

"Should we try CPR?" Susan said breathlessly.

"I'm sure it would be useless," I answered. "He's been dead for some time."

Mrs. Ryan screamed softly and buried her face in her hands. I went to her, put my arms around her, and led her out to the bench in the hall outside the door.

"Susan," I said, "Please go down to the phone and call Dr. Lev Eisenstein. His number is on the inside of the front cover of the phone book. Dr. Ben may be on duty but I think it's Dr. Lev who is needed. Tell him it's an emergency."

I felt strangely calm, Pierce had relieved me of my awful dilemma. Mrs. Ryan had unearthed her handkerchief and was sobbing quietly into it. I walked back into the room. The last time I had seen it was the day the Sheriff's men were searching. On that occasion it was far from neat, but this morning, all clutter had been stored away, the bureau top carefully polished, the bedclothes neatly arranged. A empty water glass stood on the bedside stand, along with an empty prescription vial. I didn't dare touch anything but I saw an envelope with my name written on it in Pierce's schoolboy hand and lying on the pillow beside his still face. I had to believe this was suicide and that envelope contained a farewell message. I backed out of the room and joined Mrs. Ryan on the bench, then broke down into tears.

Dr. Lev arrived and pronounced Pierce dead. He called the Sheriff on his cell phone,

"Looks like suicide," I overheard him saying, "probable drug overdose. I haven't handled the prescription vial but I think I see 'Seconal' on it. He's left a letter to Clio, probably a suicide note."

I shepherded Mrs. Ryan down to the kitchen and started her making coffee. Then I went to my room and quickly showered and dressed for the day. Normal activities would create a distraction. My eyes were too blurry with tears to get makeup on straight and my hair got short shrift with the comb, so I presented a rather haggard face when I let in the Sheriff's men. Jud Bigelow and Lieutenant Allerd arrived first, then Sergeant Ky, then the Sheriff. The drive in front of the house was lit up like Christmas, since each of their cars had been left with lights on and flashing. While they went about their procedures with Dr. Lev, I went down to the servants hall to sit with Mrs. Ryan and Susan. Mrs. Ryan had her tears under control and had started breakfast. When the maids arrived, she set them at their tasks in the first floor rooms and stopped their excited chatter with sharp admonitions.

"Being busy is best for them, and for us too," she said.

But neither Susan nor I could think of anything to do. Carter called just at 10 A.M. and when I told him what had happened, he asked no questions, offered no condolences, just said he'd be with us as soon as possible. So we helped Mrs. Ryan prepare for lunch, a welcome diversion.

When I met Carter at the front door, he wrapped his arms around me and whispered, "I'm so sorry. I know how much you loved and depended on Pierce. This is a great loss for you, perhaps more of a loss than when your father died. Tell me if there is anything I can do to make the pain and grief more bearable."

My hard-won composure collapsed and I boo-hooed helplessly into the lapel of his coat.

"Too many dead people," I sobbed. "Too many deaths too close together, I'm not sure I can take it."

"Of course, you can. Cry away all the tears that are in you. They'll wash out much of your pain. When you can't cry any more, you'll be able to deal with whatever comes along. Remember, you're not the only one bereaved. Help Mrs. Ryan, she's lost her partner of 25 years, with whom she shared the problems of running this household, who helped her reach decisions and solutions for the problems."

Carter's embrace was warm, his murmur comforting. I couldn't remember ever sheltering in a man's arms in all my 37 years. When I realized that, my reaction was one of surprise. Was this happening to me? Why did it feel so good? I gulped down my sobs and peered up at the tenderness in Carter's face, so close to mine. I didn't want to leave his embrace but I nevertheless slowly disengaged from it to avoid Jud Bigelow's curious stare. Jud was clumping down the stairs carrying a lumpy plastic bag, probably containing evidence from Pierce's room. We went on down to the servants hall where Mrs. Ryan, occasionally dabbing at her eyes, stood over a skillet of scrambled eggs. Susan was tending the toaster and pouring juice. She welcomed Carter with a nod and waved us to seats at the table. Carter, sitting on my left, reached for my hand and held it while I ate. The toast was already buttered so to my unspoken bliss I didn't have to let go.

§ Forty One §

When Sheriff Land made an appearance, he was carrying the envelope Pierce had addressed to me. It was smudged with fingerprint dust but still sealed.

"Ms. Clio, I think it's time for you to open this envelope. I very much hope you will share the contents with me. They may well be the key to all of our investigations at Hauteville House."

Wordless, I took the envelope from his hand, and stifling my tears, slit it open with my unused table knife. The page inside was close-written in Pierce's careful script:

Dear Miss Clio,

Please forgive me for what I am doing. But I've decided it's the right thing to do. I know you had nothing to do with Horace Elder's murder because I was the one who did it. I just can't bear you being accused of it and this seems the best way to avoid that. The sleeping pills I had made it easy to get close enough to put the dagger in just right and without any fuss. When the police were searching everywhere for drugs, the pills were in my pocket. I have served faithfully and honestly in this house man and boy for sixty three years. I knew your father and grandfather and your mother and did their bidding cheerfully and willingly. I watched you grow up beautiful and healthy and clever and <u>lonely</u>. Your Papa was wrong to keep you tied down so long but there was *nothing Wilma and I could do about that. Please tell her I'm sorry. We've been partners for such a long time, I think she might be grieved that I'm running out on her. We knew Elder was probably cheating Mr. Armand, servants in the house always know more than anyone thinks they know, and when I overheard you and the others in the library putting it to him, I just couldn't bear it. I had to get him out of your life if you were to have a life. I'm just sorry that the way I took has caused so much trouble. Now I'm going to drink up all the sleeping medicine in one draft and lie down to sleep forever. I wish you and Wilma many happy years to come. You have good friends and honest friends to support you now. That Mr. Evans is a gentleman and won't let you down.*

Very sincerely yours, George Alan Pierce

P.S. My keys are in the top drawer of the bureau.

I handed the letter to Sheriff Land and asked him to read it aloud, then subsided in tears again on Carter's shoulder. Mrs. Ryan was weeping softly and Susan, undemonstrative Susan, had put an arm around her and was whispering "There, there." When Land finished reading and folded the page and re-inserted it into the envelope, Mrs. Ryan wiped away her tears and spoke, "He wasn't well, you know. He suffered from a pain in his chest. I know he went to the doctor over in Deerfield but when I asked him what the doctor said, he said it was indigestion and the doctor had given him pills for it. He was a private person and I always respected that. I didn't ask any more questions. I don't know why he was taking sleeping pills for indigestion but I don't understand medical things at all."

Sheriff Land asked me, "Ms. DeVille, may I take away this letter? It's evidence until the coroner's inquest sits. Then you'll have it back. If you like, I'll get you a copy of it to look over in the meantime. There are still some questions to be resolved and I or Dr. Lev will let you know what we find out."

While I was nodding my assent, Susan was talking, "Sheriff, if it will help, I learned last night that the pills apparently came from a pharmacy in Deerfield. I'll put you in touch with the PI who reported that to me."

Land thanked her and left. The mournful parade of the coroner's men with their gurney and its shrouded occupant, Jud, Sergeant Ky, and Lieutenant Allerd passed through the hall and out the door to Dr. Lev's van, while Carter and I, Susan and Mrs. Ryan, and the maids summoned by Mrs. Ryan from their work, stood respectfully by. The maids were sniffling and wiping their eyes on their aprons. They had not known Pierce long and perhaps were a little afraid of him (he had a sharp eye and a quick reprimand for some task too casually done). I found myself hoping to God this was the last such parade through this hall for many a year. Too many dead people, too many deaths in too short a time—I dissolved into tears again, and Susan led me up to my bedroom where I could weep as hard and noisily as I wanted to.

§ Forty Two §

BY DINNERTIME I was cried out and I went down to the servants hall dry-eyed. I found Mrs. Ryan in high dudgeon because Carter had ordered in a catered meal from the village.

"Hmph," she was snorting. "I may be sad but I'm not helpless. I'll warrant the stuff that they come dragging in won't be as good as anything I can do on my worst day. Cold, for sure, won't heat up well…."

Carter was trying to tease her out of her ill humor by placing an order for a home-made, full-dress, roast beef and gravy dinner for tomorrow evening. He promised to select the wine from the House cellar, boasting he was a rather good sommelier as a result of his European experiences. She stopped grumbling when the food arrived from the Chicken Palace, bundled up in heat-retentive covers for hot stuff and insulated wrappers for cold stuff. Opening it was like Christmas morning, and she supervised setting it out with a sharp eye to its quality.

"Doesn't look bad, smells good, but we'll see when we eat it," she said grudgingly as we sat down.

Well, all of it turned out to be pretty tasty and even Mrs. Ryan partook heartily. Fried chicken, mashed potatoes, milk gravy, biscuits with butter and honey, coleslaw, and a Boston cream pie from the Eisenstein bakery. The topic of conversation was the plan for Pierce's funeral arrangements. Mallory of Deerfield was the choice and a coffined interment in the family cemetery was the plan. Susan volunteered to assist me with the invitations to the service and reception. Mrs. Ryan told us Pierce had often said he was the last of his family and that he had heartily (though tactfully) disapproved of Papa's cremation.

"He always said God didn't intend his children to go up in flames. Too much trouble to reassemble them on Judgment Day."

That wry humor gave us a cheery moment. We went on to make up a guest list and Mrs. Ryan said she would plan the buffet for the reception if I would make the arrangements with Reverend McLinn and Mallory. I ordered a simple but dignified coffin and a spray of roses, and instructed Mallory to place it in the drawing room for visiting prior to taking it to the family cemetery for burial. The reception would occur after the graveside service. I asked Reverend McLinn to limit the service in the House to a few words from the Psalms and Gospels and to use the Anglican committal service at the grave. Mrs. Ryan and I undertook the sad duty to clear out Pierce's room. We packed up his clothing and shoes to send to the GoodWill in the village. When we began to work through the drawers of his bureau, we found a surprising number of mementoes of my young life: a home-made valentine heart from a five year old, pompous essays on historical topics written by a ten year old, uninspired daubs of art work that he must have rescued from the trash, a postcard I sent him from a seaside vacation taken with one of the governesses. The message on the postcard, straggling in clumsy block print, was "WISH YOU WUZ HERE!" As I read it and flipped it over to a cartoon of a little girl with a large crab attached to her big toe, I did indeed wish he was here and my eyes blurred over with tears. Mrs. Ryan was more matter of fact, gathering up the few bits of male jewelry—most of them, she said, her gifts to him over the years. I happened on a birthday card she had given him just last year. Written on the back of the card was "*Whatever I got that's worth anything when I die I want Wilma to have. GA Pierce.*"

"Mrs. Ryan, I think this is a will. I'll have to show it to Susan and Carter to be sure it's valid but it certainly looks like he meant you to be his heir."

Mrs. Ryan sank down on the side of the bed, shaking with sobs and mopping tears with the handkerchiefs she had just removed from Pierce's bureau drawer. I sat down beside her and held her hand. I shared her grief but not her tears. Mine had dried up last night but the ache would remain in my heart always. When she had calmed down, we gathered the memorabilia from the drawers into a suit box we took from the closet. I found his personal papers: birth record, high school diploma, Social Security card, Medicare papers, and a checkbook and savings record for the Deerfield bank. The balances in both his savings and checking accounts exceeded $10,000. Paper-clipped to the checkbook was an envelope of receipts for certificates of deposit for thousands more. In sixty some years of bachelorhood and service at Hauteville House, Pierce had saved up a small fortune. I put the books and envelope in the box without showing them to Mrs. Ryan, she was upset enough for the moment, but I immediately carried the box down to Susan and Carter in the library. Both of them pronounced the words on the back of the birthday card a holographic will that would stand up in probate court; they had to explain to me that holographic meant hand written and signed by the testator. Carter volunteered to take on the legal chores to prove the legacy as soon as the funeral was over.

The guest list for the funeral was a short one but we had a surprising number of uninvited guests, local people who had read the funeral notice in the paper, people unknown to us but who knew Pierce. Even Ted came; our last letter to him had returned stamped "**NOT AT THIS ADDRESS**" but Jud had called his cell phone and reached him in New York City. One very distinguished elderly gentleman, a Dr. Emlyn, introduced himself to me as Pierce's doctor; he seemed to think Pierce had died of cancer. I took him aside and questioned him, learning that he had diagnosed Pierce with inoperable liver cancer in January. Pierce had refused treatment, only requesting medication to give him restful sleep, and Dr. Emlyn had prescribed Seconal.

"Mr. Pierce had not yet reached a severe stage of debility but he knew it was imminent and he wanted to meet it with a peaceful mind. I don't quarrel with terminal patients when I know they have come to a reasoned acceptance of their fate. Mr. Pierce was a gallant old fellow, determined to see his disorder through on his own, without visiting pain on his loved ones."

Dear old Pierce, the perfect servant to the end. Not ready to die until he had removed threats to the child he loved by the most drastic means he had in his grasp, *homicide* and *suicide*. The prayer I breathed over his coffin committed his selfless soul and sacrifice to the best that eternity had to offer.

The interment was blessed with beautiful, sunny weather. The majestic words of the Anglican committal service flowed smoothly in the Reverend McLinn's agreeable tenor. We came away from the graveside with a sense of peace and closure. Mrs. Ryan was all in a dither for fear there would not be enough food at the reception but it all worked out OK. After the guests left, and the maids had gone home, and Susan and Carter had departed, only Mrs. Ryan and I were left in the House and she went to her room for an early night. I found the emptiness of the House eerie. Going through the hall, I expected to see Pierce pottering around watering plants, or to hear Mrs. Bettle's steps heading for Papa's room, or Bonny's papers rustling in the library. After the almost constant traffic of people in and out during the last months, now the house was too empty, too quiet, too lonely—I wanted Carter back most of all, but I would have to wait until Saturday. I went up to bed to think about him and the future.

§ FORTY THREE §

I WAS OUT IN the parterre, planting the last delivery of perennials from the nursery. The boys had dug the holes I had indicated before they went off to mow and I was down on muddy knees, plying muddy gloves. I looked up at a hearty "Hullo" to see Ted emerging from the house. I sat back on my heels and invited him to sit on the stone wall. It was good to see his cheerful face. Mrs. Ryan and I had rattled around in the house for three days, seeing no one other than the maids and the lads working on the grounds. Hard to believe but we had run out of conversation, mostly because we carefully avoided speaking of Pierce. His empty chair at the table was just an unoccupied piece of furniture but the void it represented was enormous. I remembered how much we had enjoyed Ted's presence in the house while he was writing his book. We could use his sunny presence again.

I asked politely how his last book was going. He said it was in press, due out in August, he had reserved copies for Pierce, Mrs. Ryan, and me. A sad look passed over his face as he said, "When Pierce's copy comes just put it in the library. I'm not going to cancel it and I plan still to inscribe it to him, just as if he were still here to read it. He was a good guy; we got to be good friends while I lived in."

"What's next on your agenda?" I asked.

"We-e-ll," he drawled, "my editor is after me for a novel, something more than a travel book. He's pushing for a mystery, something Gothic. I told him about Hauteville House with all its towers and Victorian grandeur and my description took his fancy.

If I can come up with a plot, will it be OK with you if I took the House and its ambience for a background? I'd disguise it, make it spooky, you know."

"Great idea, go for it! Are you planning on staying with Jud's family while you write or are you going back to New York and to do it all from memory?"

"I was thinking of getting an apartment in the village. Sara Jane is pregnant again and I think I'm taking up space she wants for a nursery. I do want to stay around here, I like it and I've renewed a lot of old friendships."

"How are you getting around these days? Did you come out here on foot?"

"Bicycle. The royalties from my books are keeping me in clothes, shoes, and food, but don't stretch to fancy transportation."

He had picked a daisy and now sat staring at it, twirling in his hand. While we talked, I was turning over an impulse in my mind. So now I voiced it.

"What would you say to staying in the House while you're working on this novel? Mrs. Ryan and I are all alone, and we miss a man in the house. You wouldn't have to pay board and room; we could arrange time for you to write, and maybe you could do some chores around the place—polish silver, wash cars, boss the boys working on the grounds, move furniture, carry heavy things, you know—the kind of things Pierce used to do."

"I could never carry off the butler thing like Pierce, but the other jobs seem to be within my scope. Are you sure I could do you some good? I'll admit my income is not adequate to my cost of living right now and a job would be welcome, especially one with folks I know and like. However, you'd better ask Mrs. R for an OK before we come to an agreement, don't you think?"

Shucking off my dirty gloves and brushing off my knees, I said, "Let's ask her right now."

We had to walk around to the grade door and yoo hoo into the kitchen. I knew I'd get a good scolding if I entered with dirty shoes. Fortunately Mrs. Ryan was close by. I told her that I had proposed lodging and a job for Ted but needed her approval before closing the deal. Her usually expressionless face immediately bloomed into a broad smile.

"That would be wonderful! I've got a list of chores that need doing and it'll be a pleasure to cook for this boy. He always has such a hearty appetite and so many kind words for the cook. Welcome back. When can you start? Just look at the knob on this door, ready to fall off, and …."

Ted laughed and grabbed her in a hug; a hug that from anyone else would have been an affront but she just chuckled and hugged him back. I told him to put up his bicycle in the garage while I went to change my shoes and jeans. Then I drove him to the Bigelow's to pick up his stuff; there wasn't much of it. Sara Jane saw him off graciously but with barely concealed relief; I could sense plans whirling in her mind for painting his erstwhile room in nursery colors. By the time we got back to the House, Mrs. Ryan had maids attacking Mrs. Bettle's old room with brooms and dust mops and fresh linen, and turning out the bathroom cabinets to receive fresh shelf liners. She even offered to help Ted put up his things in the closet and bureau but he refused, saying laughingly his underwear was too ratty for public display. Our young maids received the news of his return with jubilation, quickly dampened by Mrs. Ryan's frown.

Dinner that evening was celebratory. The menu was heavy with dishes Mrs. Ryan remembered as Ted's favorites, chicken-fried steak, mashed potatoes and gravy, succotash, sweet pickles, and an imposing German chocolate cake. We were regaled with tales of Ted's most recent travels, complete with adventures and misadventures. After helping Mrs. Ryan clear the table and load the dishwasher, we settled in the morning room for more talk.

§ Forty Four §

Carter called to propose an excursion on Saturday, dinner at his club followed by a performance of *The Student Prince* by the Erie amateur theater company. He described it as "lightweight plot, pleasant music, an easy evening." Primed by my previous experience at his club, I thought to myself, good-o, a new dress! Mrs. Duncan obliged with a gauzy, swirly blue ankle-length number, with matching stole, and silver slippers. I decided to get out my mother's dangling diamond earrings to top off the whole creation.

When Carter drove up in the early afternoon, Ted was washing cars, clad only in cut-off jeans and hiking boots, whistling cheerfully as he soaped and rinsed. He waved to welcome Carter, and exchanged pleasantries with him, as I was getting myself into the Mercedes.

As we drove off, Carter said, "So, he's back, is he?"

"Yes, Mrs. Ryan and I needed a man around the house to tend to jobs that Pierce used to do and Ted is working on a new book. As he puts it, a ten dollar bill looks like a hundred to him, the royalties on his latest book have not been overwhelming. So he writes in the morning and does chores in the afternoon to earn room and board."

"I think you've got a soft spot in your heart for that young man, maybe even romantic feelings."

I gasped, taken aback that Carter should think such a thing. I almost sputtered my retort. "For goodness sake, he's just a kid. My romantic feelings are for an older man…."

I stopped short, realizing what I was saying. I could feel my face turning scarlet. A sidelong glance at Carter caught him with his eyes directed straight ahead down the highway. I fumbled with my dainty little beaded purse, to haul out a minuscule mirror for checking makeup.

"If you pull down the sun visor, there's a lighted mirror." Carter said in a level tone.

"Thanks," I answered.

We were silent for many miles thereafter. When we talked again, it was to comment on the traffic, the beautiful cloud pattern in a magnificent blue sky, the relative merits of rice pilaf versus baked potato as an accompaniment to steak. We managed to find enough commonplaces to last us all the way to our seats in the restaurant. Over our aperitifs, I kept my eyes studiously averted from Carter's face, still embarrassed by my gaffe. But quick glances from time to time detected faint puzzlement under his rather sober façade. Finally, reaching across the table to take my hand in his warm grasp, he broke the silence.

"Clio, I don't want you to worry about what you said. I'm honored and flattered if you have any special feelings for me. But I don't want them to arise out of gratitude or because your father failed to show affection for you, or because in losing Pierce you have lost a father figure. The longer I have known you and enjoyed your company, the more fond of you I have grown. I insist I'm innocent of ulterior motives, your wealth has no attraction for me, your grand house has no particular appeal, your person, as attractive as it is, rouses no sexual itch. I hope you are not insulted by that last. I find you very attractive for yourself. You are like an awakened child, facing the day with anticipation and excitement, waiting for new things to cross your path and come in your door. I must admit I love that child and want to put my arms around her. But I'm not sure I love the woman or that the woman loves me in a meaningful way. Could we not go on for a while in affection and respect, while we learn more of ourselves and one another in this relationship so new to each of us? What do you say?

I gulped, fighting back tears. If I wept I'd have to excuse myself to the ladies' room to repair my careful makeup. Then I thought how silly I was being, how gracious and kind Carter was, how sensible his solution for our situation was—and my tears dried up. When I spoke, my voice was shaky, but my words came out clearly.

"I say, thanks for giving me a way to deal with this phase of my life. I'd love to love you but I agree that feelings like that ought to go on the back burner for now. Let's just like and enjoy liking, if that's OK with you."

"It certainly is. Now, let's put that poor waiter out of his misery and order. He's hovered long enough."

Simple pleasure in dinner, the opera, and in being together describes the evening. It was, of course, late when we arrived back at Hauteville House. Carter was staying over and we said goodnight on the second floor landing. He took me in his arms and rather hesitantly kissed me on the lips I wanted to kiss back but didn't quite know how, so I patted his face briefly and disengaged myself from his embrace. He went to his room and I went to mine. I don't know how well he slept but I slept like a baby.

§ Forty Five §

The next day, Carter and I settled on a time to call on the financial advisor we had retained to evaluate my inheritance. We decided on the following Thursday and Carter said he would set up the appointment. Before Carter left for home, we took a leisurely stroll in the woods, speaking lightly of nondescript topics, but not alluding to events of the previous evening. I saw him off with a wave of my hand and another wave, one of loneliness, in my heart. But I consoled myself that I would be seeing him again soon.

It was a sign of my new found independence that I drove my own car to meet Carter at his office prior to keeping our appointment. I managed the highway without any qualms but the city traffic worried me enough to be grateful that Carter was driving us through city streets. Mr. Winkel's office was in his home, a mustard-colored Prairie style house with lots of clerestory windows and an intricate wrought iron gate between the top of the walk and the door. There was no doorbell button, but Carter reached inside the grill and tugged on a dangling rope. Distant bells rang a rather charming tune and a gnome appeared at the inner door, peered at us, and then released some kind of catch to allow us to pass the gate. It turned out that the gnome was the distinguished economist, Mr. Augustus Winkel. I was struck with his resemblance to the photos I had seen of Einstein—same flyaway white hair, bushy eyebrows, serene gaze beaming through the round lenses of his glasses. His small stature was not due to deformity; he was just unusually short. He was shod in carpet slippers.

"Follow me," he said, as he shuffled ahead of us down a long undecorated hall to a huge room where a ceiling coffered in glass poured daylight down on batteries of television screens, computers, copiers, and printers. A folder of documents lay on a bare table with three chairs disposed around it, and with a graceful gesture, Winkel invited us to sit. Carter introduced me and Winkel acknowledged me with a pleasant nod and a courteous half-bow. He seemed to be a man of few words.

He began by taking the documents from the folder, dividing them into three piles, and laying them neatly on the table between us. Looking at me, he said,

"These are the notes I have made in my evaluation of your holdings. I have divided my analysis into GOLD, SILVER, and LEAD lists."

He continued, placing his hand on each pile in turn, "The GOLD list consists of superior quality investments, among them treasury notes, government bonds, high-grade mutual funds, and triple A municipal bonds. The GOLD list also includes gilt-edged stock certificates, many of them in rock-solid utilities. All these holdings are yielding excellent returns and promise to continue doing so. I recommend you keep them and even move liquid funds into more of them. The trust fund in the National Bank of Columbus also falls in this category; I found it well-managed. Have you any questions so far?"

I shook my head no. He went on,

"The SILVER list consists of stocks which have been, and may continue to be, reasonably sound investments. The portfolio, however, is not sufficiently diversified, and has not performed well in the past few years. I have made specific recommendations for consolidating some of the holdings, selling certain of them, and replacing them with GOLD quality purchases. These holdings have been mismanaged in the past three years; their history, as provided to me by Mr. Harvill, indicates too many unprofitable sales and overly expensive purchases. Management of these holdings should be turned over to a knowledgeable broker with instructions to bring them into line with best practice."

He brought his hand down with a thud on the third pile, the LEAD list. His voice grew almost angry. "These are examples of really terrible judgment applied to financial management. Some shares are barely worth the paper they are printed on. They smell of purchases decided by locker room rumor and negotiated by unscrupulous brokering. I should not be surprised if fraud did not enter into the acquisition of some of them. They should be cleared out, sold for whatever they might bring—which I assure you will not be much. On the positive side, getting rid of the stuff that is not downright fraudulent and taking the loss will reduce your taxes. Again, these should be placed in the hands of an honest and capable broker who can liquidate them efficiently and reasonably quickly. I suggest you give such a broker *carte blanche* to use any legal and moral means to get rid of them."

He looked at me expectantly and now I had a question.

"Can you tell me that my inheritance, in the main, has not been ruined nor severely affected by Horace Elder's mishandling of it?"

"Well," he said kindly, "it's scarred, scratched, and slightly dented but in the main, it's still a very large fortune, and capable of returning a very large income, even before the SILVER and LEAD corrections are made." Then, turning to Carter, he asked, "I believe you have verified the real estate holdings that form part of the inheritance."

"Yes," Carter said. "Hauteville House and the estate, although somewhat rundown, are free and clear of debt or attachments. I understand that Ms. DeVille intends to make general repairs of the buildings and some restoration of the grounds. She will be interested to know that funds will be available for that."

Winkel assured me reorganization of the securities would not affect my disposable income adversely. He suggested I retain Mr. Harvill as my accountant, considering that Bonny had an excellent grasp of the extent and character of the DeVille holdings.

"Where," I said, "will I find a knowledgeable and honest broker who can follow up on your recommendations?"

The gnome allowed himself to smile and his eyes to twinkle as he answered.

"If you find my advice acceptable so far, I would be willing to offer my services. For references I can put you in touch with people at the New York Stock Exchange and the Trust Department of Chase Manhattan Bank—or whatever its name is now. My fees are reasonable, in line with others in my profession."

"Where do I sign?"

Carter and Winkel made the formal arrangements. We made an appointment for the following week for me to go over in detail the changes that Mr. Winkel would make. I left with a three-page summary of his specific recommendations, homework to prepare for the meeting. I breathed a deep sigh of relief. This seemed a significant start on resolving the mess Elder had got the DeVilles into. As we left, I accepted Carter's invitation to lunch. We ate at his favorite streetside café, just sandwiches and salad, but finished with ice cream desserts topped off with hot fudge and fresh raspberries—at least I had one of those desserts. Carter was content with a dish of sherbet. I was learning that he was rather conservative in the amount and type of food he favored. I decided to store that information up for future use—I hoped.

§ Forty Six §

Over the next few weeks, Carter and I spent a good bit of time together, on business and on pleasure. The business was winding up and I was almost entirely in charge of DeVille affairs. Although my command was a bit shaky, conversations with Carter and Susan helped me to make decisions and to keep me out of legal or financial trouble. Augustus Winkel's advice and action now had most of the investments in order; I was secretly proud that I had understood and participated in the reorganization—another sign of growing control of my own life. Susan, pursuing a complicated trail through Elder's manipulation of bank accounts jointly registered in his and my names, was gradually clarifying that situation. It took her and Bonny a lot of work comparing dates and amounts of securities sales in the Elder records with dates and amounts of deposits in the bank records of the two accounts. The emerging pattern seemed to indicate more than coincidence for the transactions, but unfortunately no concrete evidence of a cause-and-effect relationship.

My frequent business trips to Erie to confer with Winkel or Susan had given me passable ability to negotiate city streets and to find my way about. I often met Carter for lunch and a matinee or dinner and he came less often to spend the night at Hauteville House. Dinner was always early so I could drive home in daylight. We had a good time together, wherever and whenever we were together; and we were close and comfortable enough that his kisses of greeting and farewell could be reciprocated. To be specific, I was learning how to kiss back. One evening, after one of those early dinners at another elegant restaurant, Carter on the spur of the moment proposed a show—a performance of *Hamlet* by a highly regarded touring company. I really wanted to see it, but I demurred by reason of late hours for driving home to the House.

"Well," Carter said rather tentatively, "you could always stay over at my place. We can stop at a drug store and pick up a toothbrush for you."

Wow! I thought, this could be a new phase in our relationship. I didn't hesitate.

"Good idea. Just let me call Mrs. Ryan so she won't worry."

I could hear the surprise in Mrs. Ryan's voice but she just heard me out and signed off with an injunction to enjoy the play and to drive carefully tomorrow morning on the way home. I did wonder for a moment what her private thoughts might be but decided not to worry about them. Wasn't I a grownup after all?

Tutors had thoroughly grounded me in appreciation of the Shakespearean tragedies, from *Julius Caesar* to *Lear*, and to some extent I had enjoyed them as the written word. But I was bowled over by the stage performance. The set was stark and minimal, the costumes 17th century, the acting passionate and the diction crystal clear. I bubbled blissfully, all the way recalling highlights, as Carter drove us to his house. I finally subsided, still breathless with wonder and delight when we arrived.

He lived in a reclaimed neighborhood in two tall old brownstones that had been thrown together, gutted, and redesigned for his business quarters on the first floor and living quarters on the second and third. The only disadvantage, he said, was that local scarcity of parking had required paving what had once been the back garden as a car park. So instead of entering the house through the imposing front door, we came in by way of the alley and a functional but unimpressive back door. The first floor was nicely furnished with a reception area and cubicles with ergonomic chairs and up to date electronics. An attractive spiral stair led to the second floor and a handsome antique door studded with brass hardware. But when that door opened! I was so taken by surprise I could hardly speak. The room we entered occupied the full width of the second floor and opened at the back to a formal dining area and kitchen. A scarlet area carpet spread on polished hardwood floors and black leather divans bulked large and welcoming. Chunky glass and chrome tables accented the divans; brilliant abstract art on the walls drew my astonished gaze, as did marvelous sculptures standing on a pair of tall Chinese chests enameled with gold and green dragons. What I could see of the dining area was done in cool Asiatic colors, with more art, here delicate Japanese or Chinese silk hangings.

When I had found my voice, I said (rather rudely I'm afraid), "I never in a thousand years would have thought you would live in superlatively contemporary surroundings such as these. It's gorgeous...."

I broke off as a small dark man in a neat white jacket appeared from the kitchen.

"My houseman, Julio. Julio, this is Ms. Clio DeVille, a very special friend of mine. She's staying over tonight so would you prepare the guest room for her."

To a raised eyebrow and unspoken questions, he replied, "She has no luggage, so you might look up a pair of pajamas."

Julio sketched a slight bow and waved his hand in the general direction of the kitchen counter. Another unspoken question. Coffee, tea, wine? Carter ordered hot chocolate and almond cookies, both of which were quickly made available on the coffee table in front of a divan. Something inside of me could not resist amusement at the incongruity of such homely viands in such exotic surroundings and I burst into helpless laughter. I didn't have to explain to Carter, he knew exactly why I was laughing and he joined in gleefully.

"You must have thought my comfortable adaptation to the magnficences of Hauteville House was the result of familiarity with its ambience. And so it was, I grew up in a house very similar, lots of Bostonian Victoriana, but then in my cosmopolitan life in

Europe and traveling in the Mideast and Far East, I encountered different cultures and styles. When I finally settled down in Erie, I could give my tastes free rein. Do you like it?"

"Oh, yes," I breathed, "but considering where I come from, it takes some getting used to. It's so different from carved wood paneling and stained glass windows. But, yes, I do like it."

"Enough to live in it?"

His inquiry came as a shock, I didn't have a ready answer. But he gave me a minute to think, averting his gaze and reaching to top off my cup from the chocolate pot. When I was ready, I said, "Ye-es, but ...that would depend..."

"On?" He was forcing my answer and I yielded to my true feelings for a bold answer.

"It would depend on whoever also lived in it."

He chuckled, reached into his pocket, and brought out something concealed in his closed hand.

"Would I do?" He opened his hand, disclosing a ring with a glowing red gem. "I've been carrying this around in my pocket for weeks. But now I'm proposing, asking if you would accept it as a token of engagement. I know there's a significant age difference but I think we can close the gap if you act a little older and I act a little younger. What do you say?"

Of course, I said yes, and Carter went down on one knee and slipped the ring on my finger. It was way too big but he promised a trip to the jeweler as soon as possible for proper sizing. For the moment I failed to buy into the bargain to act a little older—I was like a kid on Christmas morning—all my dreams coming true—the star from the top of the tree on my left hand. We spent a cozy hour on the divan, speaking little, simply enjoying the embrace. I fell asleep, the victim of my country girl habit of early rising. I was only partly aware when Carter picked me up and carried me to the guest room bed, covered me with the duvet, gently kissed my forehead, turned out the light, and closed the door. I woke around two A.M. and lay in a half-dream of euphoria until I realized I was still dressed and wearing my shoes. Then I got up, undressed, hung up my clothes, and put on the pajamas I found laid out on the foot of the bed. Back under the covers, I snuggled into a delightful cocoon, then slipped away into a contented doze and on into deep and dreamless sleep.

§ Forty Seven §

DAYLIGHT PEEPED IN the window when a light knock on the door announced Julio carrying a tray with a steaming mug of coffee. Placing the mug on the bedside table without a word, he made a slight bow, and left. When I went into the bathroom, I found the toothbrush we had purchased last night laid out next to a tube of toothpaste and a voluminous woolly caftan hanging on the back of the door. Bare minimum of personal hygiene accomplished, I donned the caftan and ventured out. Carter was sitting in robe and slippers at the dining table, and as I entered, waved a wordless command at Julio in the kitchen. He jumped up to give me a big hug and a tender kiss, before seating me beside him. Julio set out orange juice, and a plate of bacon, scrambled eggs, and toast, followed by a fresh cup of coffee. I rose to the occasion and tucked into breakfast with a lumberjack's appetite. With my second cup of coffee, I leaned back in my chair with a contented sigh. Carter chuckled and took my hand,

"I presume you slept well," he said. "I know I did. I've been in a frightful stew for the last few weeks, trying to decide whether it was time to ask you. Now that I have your answer, sound sleep is a given. You see, I wasn't sure you were ready for the question although I was sure I was ready to ask it. You've made me so happy, I'm fit to burst!"

There was actually a blush on his handsome face. His usual poise was completely swallowed up in his boyish joy. I felt honored and humbled by it. I had never known such whole-hearted affection and generous love. Then I remembered I was grown up, or trying to be, and that Carter and I needed to talk about a couple of things.

"I love you, too. More than I can say. In the time I have known you, you have been mentor, friend, advisor, counselor, and now, lover. I'm overwhelmed by such a grand blessing. I'm not sure I deserve it, but I'm going to take it and revel in it. But I do have some qualms. Can we talk about them?"

"I thought we negotiated the age thing last night." Carter murmured with his lips against my cheek.

"Yes, and I'm not backing off from that bargain. But there are some other issues. I never asked and you've never said anything about children. I'm nearly 40 and the chances of …."

"Say no more. Whatever you want will be OK with me. I'm willing to let nature take its course. If you want babies, and the Lord lets us, we'll have them and love them as much as we love one another. If the Lord doesn't let us, we might adopt. If you don't want babies, we'll agree on the means to avoid it, whether it's you or me that is responsible for prevention. Hey, don't look so incredulous! I'm not being magnanimous or thoughtless, I'm absolutely open-minded on this subject. Considering our incomes, we don't have to fret whether we can afford children. Thinking of our ages, we can afford help to ease the physical strain of rearing them. I just don't see a problem."

"All right, then. I'll go along with your estimate of the situation, but I'm going to go on record that I lean toward having children, if it is possible. Now, there's another issue. We'll have two places to live, here or Hauteville House. If we can agree, we might live here during the week so you can attend to your business, but be at the House for weekends and holidays. I'm used to country living and I like it, I'm not willing to give it up entirely. What do you say?"

"Hauteville House as a country place sounds OK to me, I like it out there. However, I want to take you traveling to places I already know and love. So we needn't plan on staying at either place for long. But I should ask, would you like to travel? England, Europe, Greece, Hongkong all are possibilities."

"Oh, Oh, I've always dreamed of seeing places like that, palaces and ruins, the Mediterranean, the pyramids.... And to see them with you, what a joy that will be."

"Not to change the subject," Carter said, looking fondly into my eyes and smoothing my hair, "but how soon can we have the wedding? Pardon me for being coarse but now that I have you engaged to me, I'm all agog to bed you."

I blushed red as a beet, and ducked my head into his shoulder, not from embarrassment, more from anticipation that I would at last find out in practice what I knew in theory as a result of the carefully worded sex education that my last governess had divulged. I wasn't ashamed of being a 37-year old virgin but...

"Carter, you should know, I am absolutely inexperienced in that area. You may be disappointed...."

"Shh, shh, what you don't know, we'll learn together. I've never been much of a Romeo, but I was married, and I've had an adventure or two over the years. Nothing serious or long-term, nothing to feel guilty or to brag about. However, I'm not going to confess my sins to you or to anyone else."

This topic was not interesting to me so I switched to one that was.

"I'd like to be married at Hauteville House. I don't hate it any more and we could invite all those good folks who have known nothing but funerals there. Would that be OK with you?"

"Sure," his answer came quickly, "but *when* is more important to me than *where*!"

I told him I couldn't say until I conferred with Mrs. Ryan and Reverend McLinn.

"How big an affair are you planning?" he asked cautiously.

I could tell he was dreading a lot of pomp and circumstance. So I gave him a quick hug and assured him I wanted something simple. I was not one of those women who had spent years of spinsterhood planning a grand triumph at the altar. Marriage had never even crossed my mind as a possibility until I fell for Carter. But now excitement was rising, I was champing at the bit to start on preparations. I disengaged myself from Carter's arms to go dress for my drive back to the House. Then I remembered, my car was still at last night's restaurant. Carter hurriedly dressed and drove me there and I shared a long impassioned kiss with him before I started home. A dreary drizzle of rain was masked in a rose-colored fog.

§ Forty Eight §

I BURST INTO THE servants hall to find Mrs. Ryan, Ted, and the maids sharing lunch. I announced my news in joyous tones. Wrapping her arms around me, Mrs. Ryan's usual composure collapsed into happy tears. Then Ted grabbed me and waltzed me around the kitchen, while Lily and Clara clapped their hands to set the tempo.

"I knew something was up when you called last night. I said to Ted he's going to pop the question. You just wait and see!"

Mrs. Ryan was triumphant that her prediction had come true; then her smiles conquered her tears, and drying her eyes, ever practical, she inquired whether I had had lunch. I told her I was too excited to eat but I was willing to start planning a wedding right away. Ted, appointed himself secretary to the planning committee, and hastened to pull out a pad and pencil to start the list of THINGS TO DO. The girls clamored to start a guest list for a shower they wanted to throw. I was able to talk them out of a shower. I had few women friends to invite, and I didn't want or need shower gifts. I convinced them to put their suggestions to work on a bang-up wedding reception to which we would invite all our good friends and neighbors, and yes, the girls were to bring dates.

The next two weeks passed in a flurry. The McLinns were engaged for the service and piano accompaniment, Mallory was contacted to supply white folding chairs to be set up in the drawing room, the front hall was cleared and the floor waxed for dancing. Sally Vernon's brother's trio was hired to provide the dance music from a perch on the second floor landing. Mrs. Ryan raided Flowers R' Us for potted palms and potted flowers (justifying the expense because they would stock the renovated conservatory after), and reserved cut flowers by the bale to decorate every otherwise unoccupied flat surface. Ted bemoaned blackened hands, the result of extensive silver polishing, but cheerfully toted and lugged whatever Mrs. Ryan wanted toted and lugged. I and the red bug kept the road to the village hot picking up satin ribbon and Scotch tape and such. The maids did up guest rooms for Susan LeMoine, Marcus Atwater, Thomas Gordon, and Augustus Winkel. Bonny Harvill taught me how to use the fancy fonts in my computer to do the wedding invitations and envelopes.

Finally, to Carter's great satisfaction, the date was set for September 15. The three days before were devoted to preparation of the viands to be laid out in the dining room for the reception after the ceremony. With the kitchen a hive of activity, even I was pressed into service to stir sauces and chop vegetables and stuff deviled eggs. My wedding dress, to the scandal of Mrs. Duncan, had been made by a seamstress in the village; it was a copy in white dotted Swiss of my mother's satin confection of Chantilly lace and flounces, which, having been stored in a trunk in the attic, we found transformed into mouse nests. The seamstress had to go by a photograph but her copy was eminently successful. Mrs. Duncan was somewhat mollified by my choice of white satin shoes and a complete outfit of handmade French underwear and flounced petticoats. To her mind, French lingerie went in a small way to compensate for dotted Swiss. I refused to wear a veil, too much of a nuisance, but I did plan to wear Felicia's narrow diamond bandeau; it was a pretty but unpretentious bond to the mother I never knew .The day before the wedding the dress hung in lonely splendor in the master bedroom—yes, in Papa's room, in the very room where I had spent so many dreary hours, feeling sorry for myself, hating Papa, hating the room, hating the House. In the weeks after Papa's and Elder's deaths, we had cleaned the wall paper, scoured the floors, and polished the furniture, replaced drapes and carpets, and rearranged the furniture more attractively. I felt like I had thrown out the hate along with the grime and dust and made the room fit for happiness. I was determined to spend my wedding night in it. Maybe as a form of revenge, or penance, or something.

The day came, one of those crisp fall days of brilliant sunlight, startling blue skies, and white clouds. Jack Frost had nipped the leaves in the woods with an early touch so that the yellow, red, and brown of the hardwoods glowed in the sun among the green of the conifers. The flower beds and parterres were still bright with late blooms. Indoors, the scent of furniture polish competed with that of cut flowers. Lily and Clara had insisted on a white satin bow on the back of each of Mallory's white folding chairs and had tied every one of them in place. Mrs. Ryan helped me dress, wiping away an occasional tear. She had laid aside her stiff black silk working garb for dark green taffeta, the better to highlight the white orchid corsage I insisted she wear in her role of "sponsor" of the bride. I assumed that Carter was donning his smart blue suit under the supervision of Tom Gordon, who would be entrusted with the rings. Carter was also coaching Tom in the words of the wedding toast. Both of us had voted against formal attendants, although I had asked Mrs. Ryan to stand by to hold my bouquet of scarlet roses during the exchange of rings. As the tall clock struck 12, Reverend McLinn began to read the lovely words of the Anglican wedding service, Mrs. McLinn playing softly in the background, while Carter and I recited our vows. Susan LeMoine had grown very thoughtful when she had heard that we were promising to "obey" one another, I imagined because she was taking notes for a similar exchange of vows in her future. Whether she could bend her independent spirit to spousal obedience was yet to be seen, but the way she and Tom looked at one another these days made it possible, if not probable.

It was a joyful crowd that gathered around the buffet in the dining room and then disported itself under more white satin bows tied on the stair rail and chandeliers in the hall. Carter and I opened the ball with a dreamy waltz. Finally, I thought, the lessons in which Monsieur Michel had painstakingly drilled me when I was sixteen were paying off. It was a good thing I had been well-taught; I was, of course, expected to dance with every man who asked and I loved it. Marcus Atwater seemed to have set a goal to step out with every female at least once, but finally had to retire to sit down to mop his beaming face with a huge silk handkerchief. Ted ran him a close second, although he and Marcus both had been somewhat stressed to get their arms around Sara Jane Bigelow and Evvy Stark, each in an advanced stage of pregnancy. Mrs. Ryan had hired a caterer's staff to keep the buffet stocked with food and drink and to circulate with refills to those who preferred eating to dancing. Although Julio had been invited as a guest, he unobtrusively helped the waiters. Augustus Winkel twinkled from the sidelines, leaving his chair only once and then to take Mrs. Ryan through a very respectable two-step. Mrs. Duncan and Sally Vernon had brought along their husbands and related to all who would listen how they had brought my appearance to the peak of perfection. The trio on the landing acquitted itself very well—just the right mix of golden oldies, Beatles classics, and soft rock favorites. Lily and Clara and their *beaux* danced to everything with contemporary wiggles and stomps to which I couldn't even give a name.

By six o'clock, the buffet was depleted, the dancers were drooping but happy, and Ted brought out the champagne. He popped the corks and Mrs. Ryan poured. When each of the guests had his or her glass, Tom Gordon proposed the toast.

"To Clio and Carter, long life and happiness together. To the company here gathered to honor their union, *A votre santé.*"

Then in a flurry of congratulations from the guests and thanks on our part, Susan caught the bouquet, and Carter and I ascended the stair arm-in-arm to begin our life together. Never before had I climbed that stair with such joy.

The hate was gone forever from Hauteville House.